BRAD BATEMAN; BRAT RATMAN

Dedicated to
Christopher Marshall Ernst,
our loving son.

You made friends wherever you went.

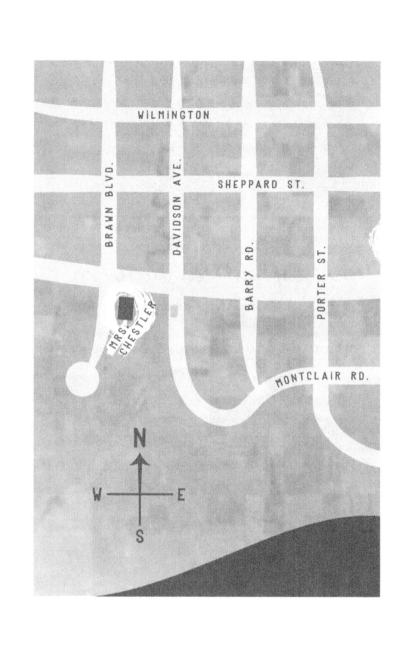

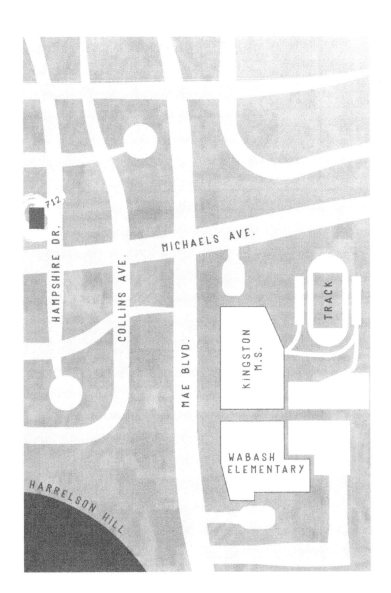

CHAPTER 1
FRIDAY, OCTOBER 31, 1993
AFTER SCHOOL

It was Friday, October 31-- Halloween day. Brad Bateman stood alone inside the boys' bathroom at Kingston Middle School. He couldn't believe he'd gotten away as easily as he had. He stood still, a little afraid his breathing could be heard.

Brad figured the guys were so busy running to the elementary school next door to "freak the little kids" that they wouldn't even notice he wasn't with them. Still, Brad looked at the door, expecting to see Arnie in his stupid Walking Death costume slamming the door open. But nobody was there. Slipping into the bathroom while the guys were throwing papers everywhere in the hall had been a smart move on Brad's part.

Brad turned to the mirror. He was immediately embarrassed by what he saw. He wanted to instantly remove the moussed hair, the white-white skin, and the dried "blood" on the corners of his mouth. Only the red from his blood-shot hazel eyes was real. The costume that his ninth-grade sister, Frannie, had said would be "sooooo cool" was now just a mess. Brad didn't want to scare little kids, he didn't want to go trick-or-treating, he didn't even want to be with his friends right now, and he definitely did not want to look like *this* anymore. Brad gave the paper towel roll a firm tug, then started scrubbing.

The paper towels felt like burlap. It reminded Brad of the gunny sack races at church camp that summer. His face was getting red from the scrubbing, but it blushed even brighter as he remembered tripping in that race. He had worked hard to hop right next to Brittany Hutchinson, the cutest girl at camp. Brad had glanced over to see if she was watching him, when HUMMPH! down he went. His face had been buried right in that burlap.

Brad jumped as he heard the bathroom door open. But instead of Arnie Sutter, Rudy Castillo, and Curt Compton, it was the custodian, Mr. Murphy. He was looking back, trying to navigate the mop and bucket through the door. Brad put his Denver Broncos hat on over his starchy brown hair and turned to go.

"Oh, hi, son. Didn't 'spect to see anyone here still," Mr. Murphy said.

"Yeah, well..." muttered Brad.

"Figured you couldn't wait to get outa here like everyone else."

"That's what I'm doing," Brad said, as he slipped by the bucket and out the door. Feeling like maybe he'd been rude, Brad waved weakly and muttered, "Happy Halloween..." before letting the door close.

He expected to see his friends leaning against the lockers, arms crossed, as he went into the hall. All he saw, though, was black and orange crepe paper strewn around. Some of it hung from the ceiling. Most of it was on top of the lockers and around the floor. Candy wrappers and crumpled up notebook paper added to the mess. Brad quickly moved down the hall, pushing the metal bar with both hands as he shot out the door.

As he crossed the bike rack area, Brad was amazed how fast a school could be emptied. He had kind of a lonely feeling as he started to walk home. Still, Brad told himself, he'd choose this over being with the guys right now. He had gotten a bad feeling before he arrived at school that day. Arnie and Curt had knocked on his door that morning and hadn't even said hello before they started bragging about how many younger kids they were going to scare. When Brad heard that, he started thinking of ways to get out of being with them. He knew if that's how things started, that Arnie would be sure to do his best to keep things moving beyond that.

2

Brad thought about saying he had a dentist appointment. But even Arnie would be smart enough to know that nobody went to the dentist *before* having Halloween candy. He thought he could tell them he was going to help Nathan Fenton with his paper route again. But just as Brad was about to say something, he remembered that Nathan had given his route to Ashley Sherman. The same Ashley Sherman who had a horrible crush on Brad since first grade. There was no way he was going to tell the guys he was helping her. So Brad said nothing. He tried to look excited when he felt one of the boys looking at him. But inside Brad had that gnawing feeling in his stomach that he had felt so many times since the beginning of middle school.

CHAPTER 2
FRIDAY, OCTOBER 31
AFTERNOON

When Brad left the school grounds, he felt his neck shiver as he heard distressed noises. Looking in the direction of the panicky sounds, he saw Arnie chasing two little kids. One of the boys screamed and then fell on the sidewalk. Arnie had to jump to avoid tripping over him. Brad started toward the boy. But then he stopped. If he went over there he would have to face his friends, which he didn't want to do. The little boy started crying. A woman, who was with three other small kids, crossed Mae Boulevard to help. When she could tell that the boy wasn't hurt, she turned toward Arnie. But he was already half a block away. He was laughing so loudly that Brad could hear him. Brad turned, shaking his head, and continued walking on Montclair Road toward his house.

Brad glanced back a couple of times on the way home. Once he thought he saw something out of the corner of his eye. He figured his friends were going to try to scare him. But nobody sneaked up on him. Even so, he had a little shiver as he walked past the thick bushes bordering his front yard on 712 Hampshire Drive.

The phone was ringing as he walked into the two-story house. He just knew it was Arnie calling to bug him about what a *great* time they'd had after school. Arnie was always saying what a great time he'd had-- especially to people who hadn't been with him. Brad knew of several times he'd been with Arnie when Arnie himself had complained of how bored he was. Then at school he'd brag about how much fun he'd had. Brad never said anything to Arnie about this, but it always got on his nerves.

As Brad walked reluctantly to the phone, he heard Frannie answer it upstairs. He listened to find out what she would tell Arnie. But it was one of Frannie's friends, and Brad exhaled, knowing that any phone calls to him would be met with a busy signal for at least the next half an hour.

Brad dropped his backpack on the stool by the phone. He automatically walked to the refrigerator and peered inside. Nothing looked good. Then he remembered the two cupcakes and the glazed doughnut he'd had at the school party.

"Yuck," he said aloud, closing the refrigerator door.

He looked out the window into the backyard. He wondered how in the world two trees could drop so many leaves. His father had asked him on Monday to rake the leaves. He had thought about it a couple of times but hadn't done anything yet. Brad usually couldn't stand the thought of doing any work on Fridays after school, but something told him that he should at least start this job today. He went upstairs to the bathroom to rinse his sticky hair one more time. He then changed his clothes and went back through the kitchen and into the garage to grab the rake.

Brad was greeted by the familiar, stinky breath of Tripp. The bushy, mottled dog jumped in his face again, and Brad instinctively faked a throw toward the door to the backyard. Tripp leaped through the doggie door, falling for the same trick he did every time. Not everyone knew how to keep the dog from getting between their legs, though. Just last summer at their Fourth of July barbecue, his mom's sister, Aunt Margaret, went down in a painful and messy heap. His parents were especially unamused when Tripp slipped back around everyone and started to lick the beans off Margaret's legs. Brad thought for sure he was going to lose the mutt that time.

He grabbed an old tennis ball off the shelf and tucked it under his left arm that held the rake. He opened the door, and Tripp barked enthusiastically when he spied an actual ball. Brad realized the dog would have to stay in the garage, though, as leaves would go flying with every stride Tripp took while chasing after a ball.

After securing the area of the beast, Brad started in the far corner of the yard. He got a momentary shock when Tiny, the Constance's St. Bernard, bellowed at him through the slats in the wooden fence behind their yard. Just one friendly comment from Brad quieted the neighbor's dog.

He decided to make one big pile of leaves in the middle of the yard. He quickly became involved, daydreaming as he raked. Sometimes he made patterns with the leaves, sometimes designs. A couple of times he watched a single leaf get separated from the pile by the slight breeze that blew. As the pile grew, so did the pleasant smell of the leaves. Brad took deep breaths the few times he paused. The sun started to fade, but Brad didn't even notice. He was so lost in his thoughts that he jumped up and let out a gasp when he felt the hand on his shoulder.

"Hey, buddy!"

"Wha... who..." managed Brad, before he realized it was his dad.

"Wow! I never thought I'd see you so caught up in something as disgusting as work that I could sneak up on you," laughed his dad, his beard showing more red than normal with the last of the sunlight shining through it.

"Yeah, I guess I was kind of out of it."

"Let me help you finish up so you can get your costume on."

"Dad, I don't, um, I don't think I'm going..." but his dad was already walking to the house to change clothes and he didn't hear Brad.

CHAPTER 3
FRIDAY, OCTOBER 31
NIGHT

"Frannie, you are going to have to sit down and eat something," Mrs. Bateman said, as Brad was helping himself to a second hamburger.

"Mommmm, this stupid costume is just not working out!" Frannie hollered, leaping up two steps at a time toward her room. "Besides, Tanya's ordering like 20 pizzas," she added from the top of the stairs, her long, dark hair dangling over the railing.

Brad was glad the attention was on his sister. He'd been figuring out how to explain that he wasn't going trick-or-treating ever since he'd bagged the last of the leaves. He'd been thinking of this so much, that he surprised himself by answering, "Around seven," when his mom asked what time he was planning to go out. Suddenly he realized that it wouldn't be so bad going out. Arnie and the others had probably scared enough kids already after school. Besides, having a full bag of candy was not exactly a bad thing. He would go.

So it was that Brad went up to his room somewhat enthusiastically. He did not want to wear the same thing he had worn at school. His face still itched. Frannie would whine, but oh well. He thought about the classic Charlie Brown ghost idea, a sheet with a dozen holes in it. But the only extra sheets he could find were his old Power Ranger ones. Arnie would tease him unmercifully if he used those. He sat on his bed thinking. Instantly his door burst open and there was Arnie.

"What are you waiting for, Brat Ratman?" Arnie practically shouted the nickname Brad hated, as he rushed over to where Brad sat. "Let's go, dude!"

7

Brad discreetly slipped the Power Ranger sheets under his pillow, and said, "Arnie, your hair is starting to fall. You kind of look like an old lady now, not Walking Death."

Trying not to laugh, he asked, "You haven't even taken that stuff off since school?"

Arnie snapped back, "Of course not, creep. I've been busy," as he brushed his long, bleached hair out of his face.

Brad thought of all the things Arnie would see as "important" but decided not to say anything. He knew the fact that he had left his friends after school would come up soon enough, and Brad didn't want Arnie to get angrier with him.

Frannie flashed by the door, dressed up like a cave woman. Arnie started laughing and so did Brad. She stopped and looked as though she was going to say something. Then she suddenly turned away and just muttered, "Children..."

Arnie said, "Hurry up, there are tons of kids out there already!"

"What, are you afraid everyone else is going to get the good candy?" asked Brad.

"No, I'm afraid I'm going to have to drag a nerd out of his house by his nose!"

A nerd, thought Brad. It had been done a bunch of times before, but it would be easy to pull that costume together. He grabbed a handful of pens from his desk, then went to his closet for the striped dress shirt that his grandmother gave him for his 10th birthday. It was still way too big two years later. He slipped on dress pants and shoes. His dad didn't seem too offended when he asked to borrow his old glasses, "You know, the ugly ones." The electrical tape around the nose piece didn't take long, and they were ready.

"You look cute, Brad," sighed his mom as they were leaving. She reached up to hug him. He already passed her in height last year in fifth-grade.

"Thanks, Mom. I'll be back in a couple of hours."

"You be back here by 9:00- at the latest," said his dad.

"All right. Bye!" shouted Brad as he closed the front door.

Arnie reached up and pinched Brad's cheek. "You are soooo cute, little Bratty," he said sarcastically. "How can you stand having your mom talk to you like that?"

"I don't know," was all Brad said. He didn't think that was a bad comment to hear from a mom.

"Well, we're already late, so let's hurry up," said Arnie as he started to run.

"Where we going?" asked Brad, trying to catch up.

"We're going to Curt's, you dork. I already told you."

Arnie started north on Hampshire Drive, then began sprinting, which surprised Brad. Arnie had been chubby ever since preschool when they first met, and Brad couldn't remember Arnie ever running this fast. Brad ran harder to catch up, wondering what the rush was. They were almost to Sheppard Street when Brad suddenly heard, "AHHHHHHHHHHHH!" and other screams from several directions. Right there in front of him jumped several faces, yelling wildly. He felt himself being pushed, then felt a pain in his shoulder as he landed on the sidewalk. He heard more shouting and laughing. When he looked up, he recognized some faces. Arnie was right in front of him, laughing hysterically. Then he saw Curt waving his arms and jumping crazily. His short body and buzz cut combined to make him look cartoonish. As Brad started pulling himself up, he noticed Rudy. He stood back somewhat and just smiled nervously. Two more people were there, but they were back further and Brad couldn't make out their faces.

"This is too perfect!" shouted Arnie. "The nerd gets wasted by the studs!"

"Oh man, we totaled you, dude!" yelled Curt, his high voice sounding especially squeaky.

Brad was on his feet now. Feeling very much like a nerd from a movie, he searched the ground for his glasses. He saw them just as Curt was about to stomp on them as he continued his wild dance. Brad pushed Curt out of the way, knocking him into one of the other people. Brad realized it was Curt's older brother, Derek.

"Watch it, jerk!" Derek grumbled.

9

Brad didn't like getting knocked over, but he really didn't like the fact that Derek was along with them. Derek was Frannie's age. She had complained about him ever since first grade. He was always in trouble and always in fights. He hardly ever won, but that never seemed to stop him. Brad could see the other guy better now. He didn't recognize him, but he figured he was a friend of Derek's--if there was such a thing.

Brad looked at the two bigger boys. They stood out because they were taller than the others, but there was something else. Brad realized that they weren't wearing costumes, just very baggy pants and loose coats. They both had long hair tucked behind their ears. Brad felt very young and embarrassed for having a costume. The enthusiasm he had after dinner had vanished. He wished he had just stayed home.

Brad realized that Rudy was next to him but wasn't saying anything. He felt a poking in his side and saw that Rudy was handing his glasses back to him. He had on his baseball uniform. The street light cast an unusual shadow on Rudy's face. With Rudy's dark skin, it took Brad a moment to realize that Rudy had black marks under his eyes, just like the pros use to help with the sun's glare. He must have realized Brad was looking at him, because Rudy whispered, "My mom made me." Curt had on the same supposedly scary costume he wore at school.

Apparently feeling like quite a leader, Arnie said, "Well, come on, dudes, let's go!"

Derek mumbled, "Shut up. Are Ken Griffey Jr. and Dorkie ready?"

Curt and Arnie let out laughs that were obviously fake, and Arnie slapped Derek on the back. Derek turned quickly, grabbing and twisting Arnie's arm. Between clenched teeth he said, "Don't ever touch me, jerk."

Only Curt responded with his machine-gun laughter. Derek turned toward his friend, who didn't say anything, but started walking up the sidewalk. Derek quickly followed. The older boys turned to go up to the house but stopped at the door. In a voice that was somewhat deep to begin with, but was obviously pushed to its lowest limits, Derek's friend said, "Let the kindergartners stand in front."

Derek quickly replied to his friend, "Yeah, Sweet, good idea, man."

Feeling very awkward having everyone looking at him, Brad put his head down and walked up to the door. He stood there waiting, not aware that Rudy was again standing next to him.

"Well, what are you waiting for-- Christmas?" Derek laughed. His buddy Sweet said nothing, and Derek abruptly stopped smiling.

Rudy looked at Brad, and at the same time they reached for the doorbell. Brad looked up, as a woman about 50 years old answered the door. Brad had seen her before but didn't know her name. She had a big smile on her face and a bowl of Mini-Snickers in her hand. The boys stood staring for a few moments until the woman asked, "Aren't you supposed to say something?"

From the back Derek said, "No, you're supposed to give us food."

Sweet joined in with his deepest voice, "And make it good."

The woman looked past Rudy and Brad to the older boys and said, "And who are we tonight-- Darth Vader?"

Brad burst out with a laugh. The woman lowered the bowl down to Brad and Rudy, and they both grabbed a couple of the candy bars. When the other boys came forward she pulled the bowl back. "Well...?" she asked.

Curt urgently chirped, "Trickertreat," followed by Arnie. She handed them each one piece. The older boys refused to say anything, and the woman closed the door.

Sweet grabbed Rudy's bag, took out the Snickers, threw the chocolate bars in his mouth and the wrappers on the ground. Before Brad could stop it, Derek did the same with his bag. Derek handed the bag back to Brad and, with a big phony smile, said, "Thanks, Brat." The older boys crossed Sheppard, and the others followed.

11

At the corner house the younger boys all chanted out, "Trick or treat," without much enthusiasm. All six boys received candy. Brad said, "Thanks," but everyone else just walked away. Derek snapped, "You're a good little girl scout, aren't you, Nerdo?" For the first time, Sweet laughed slightly. Derek gleamed with pride.

The process continued the rest of that block of Sheppard, continuing past Porter Street, and the next block after they crossed Barry Road. Rudy or Brad would ring the doorbell and say "Trick-or-treat", the others would swoop in and grab candy as soon as it was offered. Derek's comments grew more and more obnoxious. Arnie and Curt tried their hardest to sound like him. Brad's thank-you's got softer and softer.

The group angled across Sheppard to Davidson Avenue. Brad rang the doorbell at the first house on the block. He was surprised that they each got full-sized packages of Skittles. Brad was impressed, and his thank-you was again loud enough for them all to hear. Without warning, Sweet picked up a jack-o-lantern before the door was even closed. Derek grabbed the other one, and he looked like a mirror image as he mimicked Sweet's toss of the pumpkin onto the sidewalk. The door burst open with a shout from the man, and the two older boys sped away. In their surprise the others had stood looking at the smashed pumpkins until they realized the man was coming out the door toward them. They also ran, with Brad's glasses again sliding off as he turned. He looked back at them and saw the man a few feet away. Without waiting, Brad flew.

Curt, Arnie, Rudy, and Brad didn't stop running until they were at the end of the block. Brad's chest ached.

"Oooooweeee---that was----cool!" Curt sputtered, obviously out of breath.

"Yeah ---really---cool," managed Arnie.

Brad wanted to say that he thought it stunk, but what came out was, "I lost my dad's glasses."

Trying to sound like his brother, Curt said, "Go back and get 'em, geek."

Arnie again forced his laugh.

Brad felt outnumbered. Even though Rudy hadn't laughed with the others, he was turned away from Brad. If the attention wasn't on him, Rudy wouldn't do anything to change that.

Inside Brad raged. He was angry at the idiots for throwing the pumpkins, and he was really frustrated that he'd lost his dad's glasses. Brad was sick of all the rotten comments from his so-called friends. He was disgusted with himself for having gone out on Halloween at all.

As though he was taking the only positive thing away from Brad, Arnie burst out, "Hey, where's Sweet and Derek?"

Without thinking, Brad whispered, "Gone, thank God."

Curt heard it and pushed Brad as he said, "What's that mean, twerp? You're lucky they're even bothering with punks like you."

"Yeah, real lucky," was all Brad offered.

"I mean it. What are you trying to say, Brat?" shot back Curt.

Several things flashed through Brad's mind. Each of them would have just made the situation worse, he realized.

"Nothing. Just nothing," was all that came out.

Brad knew that Curt and Arnie wanted to find the older boys. He was quite confident Rudy wasn't in a hurry for more abuse, though. Surprised that no one was saying anything yet, Brad spoke up. He was fairly sure they had run north into the dark of the church parking lot at Wilmington and Davidson.

Trying not to sound too eager, he said, "I think they went toward Brawn," which was the street west of them. Not wanting to risk going back on Davidson toward the house with the smashed pumpkins, or north toward the church parking lot, Brad started to slowly shuffle west on Michaels Avenue toward Brawn Boulevard.

Curt slapped him on the back and said, "Hey, good thinking, Brat Ratman," as he passed Brad.

They got to Brawn and saw nobody on the street. In fact, it was kind of spooky. Back on Sheppard they had seen several groups of kids, but here there were no others. Without saying

anything, the four boys looked up and down Brawn, but –
thankfully, thought Brad – there was no sign of the older boys.
They crossed Michaels and headed back east. East back toward his
house, Brad thought pleasantly. He kept walking before he realized
the others were heading up the sidewalk of a well-lit house. Brad
ran to catch up. He couldn't help but notice that all of them said
some type of a thank-you this time.

They got to the next door and Brad was starting to feel a
little better. The people were friendly, and the boys weren't rude.
They started up the sidewalk of the next home, and Brad realized it
was where Mrs. Chestler lived. He had always admired the neat
light poles that lined the curving sidewalk up the slope to her front
porch. She was a friend of his grandmother's, and he had mowed
her lawn for the past three years.

As Arnie was about to ring the doorbell, Curt picked up the
lone jack-o-lantern. Brad spun his head toward him and heard the
doorbell at the same time. Curt started his wacky dance, holding
the pumpkin above his head. The door opened, and the pumpkin
slipped out of Curt's hands. With an awful crashing, it smashed the
glass fixture above the light pole next to the porch. Without
looking, Brad flew off the porch, across the yard, and around the
hedge. He knew he couldn't ever face Mrs. Chestler if she knew he
was a part of that. Brad sprinted, just hoping she hadn't recognized
him.

He ran as fast as he could until he got to the corner of
Davidson and Michaels, where he ducked behind a van that was
parked there. He slid along the driver's side up to the front. He
didn't see the others as he peeked through the windshield. He
started back across Michaels, angling north to the other corner.

As he got to the other side, a shiver suddenly ran down
Brad's back. He realized his situation. He was alone on Halloween
night. He didn't see his supposed friends. But where had they
gone? It would be just like them to be sneaking up on him right
now. He frantically turned around - but saw no one.

He continued walking toward his house, which was still
two blocks east and a half block north. Brad thought of the two

tough guys, Derek and Sweet. What would they do if he ran into them? He hadn't exactly been on their good side all night.

Brad jumped as he heard shrill laughter. He looked up and saw that it was just a group of trick-or-treaters that had appeared from around the corner. Again, he looked behind as he started to walk. He saw no one else. A porch light went out as he walked by, adding to his nervousness. He kept walking. He kept his head down, perhaps afraid of what he might see. He picked up his pace.

When he did look up, Brad tripped on a crack in the sidewalk. He was almost to Barry Road, and he quickly checked right and left before jogging across. One more block to Porter, then to Hampshire, and half a block until he'd be home. Brad kept jogging.

Out of nowhere he heard a yell, "Braaad!" His heart skipped two beats. It came from a little south of him, but to the east. The boys were almost back on Hampshire heading for his house! He had no time to think. He sprinted the rest of the way to Porter, twice hearing his name echoing through the uneasy night. Without realizing it, he ran right onto Porter Street. He heard the screech of tires and a honk at the same time. He scarcely glanced to his right to see the car, barely 10 feet away. Brad felt guilty, but he continued his race home. He had to get there before they did. He couldn't go back to Hampshire or they'd see him. He'd have to sneak through his backyard.

The only sound came from Brad's chest, until he again heard the shrill sound of, "Braaad..adddBraddd!" this time coming from several voices at once. Brad stopped abruptly. The voices came from the same distance as before. Those idiots were running too! He pushed himself even harder.

As he came up to the Constance's house, he stopped. He walked past their front door, then the garage. Looking over their backyard fence, he could see a little of the kitchen light coming from his own house now.

He looked across the Constance's lawn. Their six-foot fence stood, sternly blocking him from the backyard. All around

15

the base of the fence evergreen shrubs taunted Brad. This would not be easy.

He took a running start and leaped up to the fence. His slick dress shoes didn't hold, and he slid down into the shrub. Brad pulled himself up and hopped through the scratchy shrub to the gate. He knew the gate would be locked, and it was. He wiggled his foot into the handle and lifted himself against the brick of the garage. Brad flung his legs over the fence. His bag of candy didn't make it over, but Brad did. In a heap.

Immediately the terrifying barking of Tiny the St. Bernard erupted in Brad's face. Louder than he thought possible, Brad screamed back in horror. He smelled Tiny's hot breath and felt drool splash across his face as the huge dog bounced back and forth. His bellowing voice shattered the last bit of calm Brad had. Tears formed in his eyes.

"Tiny! Shut up--it's me!" Brad shouted.

One tear streamed a straight path down Brad's right cheek. He took a deep breath and wiped his face with his sleeve. He sniffled back the rest and took another deep breath. Finally, he spoke quietly to Tiny, who slowed the number of barks, but not the volume. Brad discovered the bag of Skittles that had been hastily stuffed in his pocket when Sweet had thrown the pumpkin. He ripped open the bag and put it on the ground. Tiny launched his face into the candy, and Brad raced toward his fence.

The supports were on this side, and Brad used them to quickly climb over. Tripp came racing from the garage, growling. As soon as Brad called his name, Tripp jumped up and gave his usual hello bark. Brad started toward the house, but Tripp got between his legs, and down he went. Brad smacked the ground in frustration.

He got up and faked a throw for Tripp, then ran to the garage. Just as he opened the door to the kitchen, he heard the doorbell ring. He held his breath as he kept the door open a crack. Just as he feared, he made out Arnie's loud voice, "Trick-or-treat again, Mrs. Bateman!"

She responded brightly, "Well, hi again, Arnie. Curt, Rudy, hello to you boys." There was a pause, then, "O.K., Brad, now where are you hiding?"

"Isn't he here?" asked Rudy, concern sounding in his voice.

"Well, no," she said. "He left with Arnie an hour and half ago. Come on, Brad, come out now," she said, louder.

Brad heard Curt mumble, "Umm, I gotta go now."

"Now really, Arnie, where is he?" she asked, with some strain in her voice.

"I really don't know. He just took off running, and we were trying to find him. We figured he'd be here."

"Well, he's obviously not here, and we'd like to know where he is," said Brad's father, having joined the group at the door.

"Really, Mr. Bateman, we don't know where he is," said Rudy.

"He's probably on his way here right now," Arnie hurriedly said. "Curt took off, so we gotta catch him. Bye!" And with that Brad heard them running down the driveway.

Before the front door was even locked, Brad was walking through the kitchen toward his parents. They turned and saw him.

"Brad! This really isn't very funny," scolded his mom.

"Mom, it wasn't a..."

"Your mother was worried sick, Brad," interrupted his dad.

"It wasn't a joke, Dad. I just ..."

"Just what, Brad?" asked his dad.

"I just, well...I just couldn't stand being with those guys anymore!" Brad said, his voice rising as he talked.

"I'm sorry," he added quietly.

Brad started to explain about the night. He began with Arnie leading him down the street so fast. His mom winced when he told her about getting knocked down, and she came over to check on his shoulder when he said how it hurt when he landed on it.

17

"Do you want some Tylenol or a heating pad?" she asked, as she rubbed it.

"No, Mom, it's fine. Really."

Brad went on with his story. His parents both looked at each other seriously when Brad said Derek was with them.

"Now wait a minute. Who is 'Sweet'?" his dad asked when Brad continued.

"He's a friend of Derek's, I guess. I think he's the one who moved here right before school started."

Brad told his parents about the rest of the night. Except he didn't tell them about Mrs. Chestler's light fixture. Brad just said, "Then Curt dropped someone's pumpkin, and I took off."

After Brad was done, his dad spoke up, "I don't get it, Brad."

Brad worried that he wanted more details about where the pumpkin was dropped. Instead, his dad continued, "Why'd you even go? You said you didn't feel right about it from the start."

Brad shrugged his shoulders.

"What does that mean?" his dad continued, his arms crossed in front of him. "Why'd you go?"

"I don't know," Brad said, his hazel eyes looking off, "I don't know."

In a louder, irritated voice, his dad said, "Well, you better start knowing because we don't need this kind of garbage happening again."

CHAPTER 4
SATURDAY, NOVEMBER 1
MORNING

On Saturday morning, Brad rolled over in bed and thought he heard a phone ringing in his dream. He opened his eyes slightly. The bright red 8:01 on his clock seemed way too bright, and he pinched his eyes shut. He became aware of the muffled voice of his mother coming closer to his room. Her voice stopped, but the door creaked slowly open. Brad opened his mouth slightly to make it appear as though he were really sleeping. The door closed, and he heard his mom say, "He's still sleeping, Rudy, but I'll tell him you called." The voice continued, but it faded too much for Brad to hear the rest of what she said.

Brad rolled over, making sure to keep his eyes closed. He pulled the covers over his head in a vain attempt at falling back to sleep. Thoughts of last night began bombarding his head. Images of getting knocked down happened over and over. Broken pumpkins flew from right to left, then back again. Broken glass shattered repeatedly. A memory of Tiny's bark exploding in his face finally made him sit up on his elbow. Propping up his pillows, Brad boosted himself in an effort to control these ideas.

Unable to do so, he was about get out of bed when the door burst open. A very disheveled Frannie all but screamed, "Why don't you tell those annoying little friends of yours that *some* people actually sleep in on this planet, and if they need so stinking desperately to talk to you at sunrise then they're just going to need to e-mail you or send you ...Morris code, or ... just wait 'till a decent time!" With that, she slammed the door shut behind her.

Brad heard his mom's sing-song voice, "Oh, good morning, Frannie honey! How are you, Sweetheart?"

"Not fine!" Frannie ripped back, then slammed her door shut.

Brad exhaled deeply as he put his hands behind his head. "I haven't even gotten out of bed yet and I've already made somebody mad," he thought.

"What's up with Rudy calling at 8:00? He must have been worried calling so early. But he found out I'm home because Mom told him I was asleep," Brad realized. "As long as he knows I'm not kidnapped-- or lying in a bunch of pieces somewhere-- he won't have to worry anymore."

Brad's mind continued to roam, as he thought to himself, "Rudy's O.K. He's a good friend, I guess. I mean we've had a lot of fun together." Brad thought back to the camping trip he took with Rudy's whole family. It was a way to celebrate finishing elementary school, and Brad had been surprised that Rudy had invited him. He didn't think of himself as Rudy's best friend or anything, but Mrs. Castillo had told his mom, "Your darling Brad is the only boy Rudy wants to take with us," when she had called to invite him. Brad had really been treated nicely, just like he was a part of the Castillo family. They stayed for two nights and had gone fishing all three days of the trip. He and Rudy even had their own tent to themselves.

But there was something about Rudy that left Brad feeling disappointed or something. Brad thought back to third grade when he and Rudy were playing chicken fights with Arnie and Curt. He and Rudy had taken turns being carried on the other's back. Both times they had managed to knock Curt off Arnie's back, and Arnie had started to get mad. He had said something about it not being fair "because Curt is such a shrimp." Brad told Rudy that they should play one more time and purposely let the others win. Rudy agreed and Brad climbed on his back. Arnie didn't know their plan, and he was determined to win.

He came barreling at them, with Curt screaming like a cowboy on a bucking bronco. Rudy let go of Brad's legs even before there was any contact and jumped out of the way. Brad headed backward to the ground. Arnie continued like a bull and drove straight into Brad just as his hands were meeting the ground to catch his fall. Brad's left wrist took most of Arnie's force and broke immediately. Brad didn't remember a whole lot after that. But he did remember seeing Rudy running away from them. When Brad returned to school two days later, Rudy wanted to sign his cast. Brad asked Rudy why he left. Brad never forgot Rudy saying, "Chicken fights are against the rules. I'd get a behavior mark if I got caught having chicken fights." Then Rudy signed the cast without saying anything else.

After he got out of the shower, Brad headed downstairs. He'd been thinking that it was very likely that Arnie would call or, worse, come over. Arnie was so persistent. He just always seemed to assume Brad would want to be with him. During the times that Brad didn't want to be with him- which had become more and more frequent since they had started middle school- he had never been able to say no to Arnie. Arnie either said something like, "Are you too good for your old buddies?" or "Think of your friends, Brat Ratman. Quit thinking of just yourself."

Brad noticed his dad heading out the door in his running clothes. Thinking that Arnie would be coming by any minute, Brad said, "Hey, Dad, wait up."

"Morning, Brad. How ya doing?" he responded, as he mussed up Brad's still-wet hair.

"Pretty good. Um, you think I could go along with you on my bike?"

"Sure," he said, squinting just a bit as if studying his son. "I bet it's been over a year since you've come with me."

"Yeah, well, it's a nice day and all..."

"Oh?" said his dad, looking up at the threatening clouds.

Brad didn't say anything but walked over to the garage to get his bike and helmet.

His dad was stretching, his head down by his ankle. He looked upside down at Brad and asked, "Don't you want a sweatshirt or something?"

21

Brad thought it looked weird to see the reddish beard on top, as though his dad had a crewcut. Not wanting to risk any more time at home where Arnie could trap him, Brad said, "No, I'm set," despite shivering just a bit as he said it.

Brad's father clicked his timer watch and started running south. They crossed Michaels at the corner, continued south, and then headed east on Montclair. They had to wait for cars at both Collins Avenue and Mae Boulevard. Brad was thinking that this would be kind of a pain to have to keep stopping at every corner, when his dad turned over his shoulder and said, "Hope you don't mind if I run a few laps on the school track."

Brad followed his dad once around the track, then realized he probably looked kind of dorky going around and around on his bike. He'd done what he wanted by getting away from home- well, from Arnie. So, he leaned his bike on an oak tree near the track and plopped down next to it. He wished he had brought a sweatshirt, as the cool breeze picked up a bit. The tree had lost almost all its leaves, and the few orange ones left danced in the light wind.

Brad watched his dad. His long legs kept a steady rhythm. His face never changed expression. Brad never was fond of just running to run. He liked all kinds of sports and would run like crazy in a game. But he just didn't like to run like his dad did.

He started daydreaming about his last soccer game a week ago. He had almost scored a goal, but his shot missed by just a few inches. It wouldn't have changed the result; they still lost by three. But it would have been nice to have that memory to keep until spring. He started wondering about how basketball tryouts at school would go, when he was surprised by a clear, high voice saying, "Hi, Brad!"

Brad quickly sat up and said, "Hi," to Ashley Sherman, who had ridden up to him on a bike. He instinctively looked around to see if the guys were around to tease him.

"Are you waiting for somebody?" she asked.

"Ahhhh, no. I mean yes. I mean that's my dad," Brad managed, pointing to the disappearing silhouette of his father as he rounded the far turn of the track.

"Oh, cool!" she said brightly. "How come you aren't running, Brad?"

"Oh, I just wanted to ride along behind him."

"But you're not riding either," she said with a small giggle.

"No, I, um, I guess I'm not," Brad said, now feeling dorky that he *wasn't* riding.

Trying to take the focus off him, Brad asked, "You just riding around?"

"Well, actually, I just finished my paper route."

"Oh yeah, Nathan's old route, right?"

"Yep," she sighed. "Except I don't think Nathan ever overslept as bad as I did today."

Brad laughed slightly, "*You* overslept, Ashley? That must be like your first mistake ever."

Ashley blushed a little, and Brad gulped, thinking maybe he'd goofed somehow by saying that.

"Oh, I've made tons of mistakes--just today!" Ashley said. "You should have seen the look on this one guy's face when I gave him his paper. He wasn't standing on his driveway, he was clear out on the street waiting. He looked at his watch for like 10 seconds before I got to him, then made this face like he'd just eaten sauerkraut or something for breakfast!"

Brad laughed. He could just picture this old guy, his whole day ruined because his stupid newspaper wasn't there at dawn.

Ashley looked at him and smiled. Brad smiled back for a moment, then quickly turned away. He pretended to look for his dad but scanned the area for any sign of the guys.

As if reading his thoughts, Ashley said, "So did you go trick or treating with Arnie and those guys?"

Brad frowned. "Yeah." He thought about saying something about it, but she started talking again.

"Do you remember Brittany Hutchinson from church camp?"

Brad blushed when he heard her name. He just nodded yes and was relieved when Ashley continued talking.

23

Enthusiastically she said, "Anyway, I was so surprised 'cuz she called me last week. Her church did this kind of youth group thing last night, and she invited me to go. So, I went. It was so much fun! That's why I overslept this morning. They had this band there and, oh-my-gosh, like a mountain of food. It was just really great." She smiled again, and Brad caught himself looking at her longer this time.

Brad was about to say something when he heard his dad run up.

"Hello there...it's Miss Sherman, right?" Mr. Bateman said haltingly, as he subtly ran in place.

"Yes, it is. Hi!" she said.

"Actually, Dad, this is Ashley. Ashley Sherman," Brad explained.

"Oh, of course. Hal and Sheila's daughter. How is your family doing?"

"We're doing great!" she answered.

"Well good. Tell them I said hello." Mr. Bateman looked at his son a moment, then asked, "Brad, do you want to just meet me at home?" as he started running.

Brad surprised himself by starting to answer yes, but as he looked up toward his dad he saw two boys heading across the playground of the elementary school. He looked more carefully and saw that it was Curt and Derek Compton.

"Umm, no, I'm going with you," he hurriedly said. He looked over at Ashley. She was looking toward the approaching boys with her forehead creased, frowning somewhat. When she noticed Brad looking at her, she promptly smiled.

"So... have a good day, Brad," she chirped.

Brad had already gotten onto his bike, and, looking back to her, he waved and said, "Thanks- you too."

Brad started pedaling faster. He looked for his dad and realized he was heading north on Mae Boulevard, not west toward home. Brad changed directions, careful not to look right, in Curt's direction. He heard Curt holler for him but pretended not to hear him as he looked back over his left shoulder toward Mae Boulevard before crossing it.

As he pedaled, Brad thought, "Oh great! More ammunition for Curty boy. First I lose them last night, and now he sees me talking to Ashley Sherman. I can hear it now. 'You'd rather be with your *girlfriend* than your real friends, huh, Brat?'"

Brad was so deep in thought he didn't realize he'd ridden right past his dad.

"Are you setting a world record?" he heard his dad call. Brad pulled on his brakes and waited.

"Keep going. I just didn't want you to miss our turn," Mr. Bateman said breathily. "We're going to turn left when we get to Michaels."

Brad didn't remember going on this route, but his dad was right, it had been a long time since Brad had joined him. They passed Montclair then turned west on Michaels. After they turned onto the quieter street, Brad's dad stopped. He caught his breath a moment, then said, "How come you didn't stay back there, Brad? It looked like you two were having a nice time."

"Yeah, well, I was ready to go, Dad,"

"Really?"

"Yeah, sure."

"It didn't have anything to do with Curt and his brother showing up, did it?"

Brad looked up quickly, "What do you mean, Dad?"

"Come on, Brad. Why do you think I left the track? After what you told me about last night, I didn't think you'd want those two sneaking up on you."

Brad hesitated a moment, then said, "Thanks."

"Especially when you were talking to your little friend."

"She is not my 'little friend', Dad!" Brad said excitedly. "That's Ashley Sherman."

"So I heard."

"She's only had a major crush on me since I was born!"

25

Mr. Bateman was genuinely surprised when he said, "That's the same little girl who used to chase you all around at recess?"

"Same girl, Dad."

"Well, Brad, she's very nice! You know I've always admired somebody who can look you straight in the eyes."

"Dad - enough. I don't need to get it from you, too. I hear enough of that stuff from those idiots."

"Fair enough," his dad responded. Then he asked, "So what about those 'idiots', Brad?"

"What do you mean?"

"It just seems like since you started middle school you've spent as much time trying to avoid Arnie and Curt as you have spent with them. Same with Rudy- I saw you crumple up the note Mom wrote telling you that he called."

"He just wanted to make sure I wasn't lying all dead somewhere so he didn't have to feel guilty."

"Brad..."

"It's true, Dad. Rudy's nice and all, but he doesn't really care about me. He just wants to make sure he doesn't get hurt or in trouble or whatever."

"So, do you care about Rudy?"

Brad furrowed his eyebrows, then looked at his dad. "What do you mean?"

"Just what I said: Do you care about Rudy?" he repeated slowly.

"Well, yeah--course I do."

"Really?"

Growing frustrated with this unexpected questioning, Brad rather tersely responded, "That's what I said."

"That's good. Since you care about him, why not call him back?"

"He found out I made it home, that's all he cares about."

"Brad..."

"What?" Brad interrupted, his voice louder than before.

"Number one, look at me," his dad said firmly. "Number two, think about what happened last night."

"Trust me, Dad, I have about 600 times."

"What I'm saying is to look at it from Rudy's eyes. It sounds like he wasn't exactly having the time of his life either."

"So?"

"So, if Rudy was also frustrated and mad at those other guys, and then all of a sudden you were gone, don't you think that would have bothered him?"

"Maybe."

"Don't you think he'd want to know what you did?"

"Fine! I'll call him," Brad said impatiently. "Can we just go?"

His dad shrugged his shoulders and said, "Sure," before he started to run again.

Brad waited a few minutes before he started pedaling. He went slowly, purposely staying further back than he had earlier.

As they made their way west on Michaels Avenue, Brad wasn't sure what he felt. Part of the time he was mad at his dad for bugging him, then he was mad at Curt for showing up. But why would he want to stay and talk to Ashley anyway? And man! Brittany Hutchinson called her? Why couldn't *he* have gone to that deal last night?

Brad instinctively turned right when he got to Hampshire Drive, expecting to see his dad heading home. He didn't see him though, so Brad circled back to Michaels Avenue. "Why is he crossing Porter?" Brad asked out loud, seeing his dad a full block ahead. He continued running past Barry and Davidson.

Brad pedaled hard to catch up. When Brad got even with his dad he asked, "Dad, are you heading back soon? I'm kind of cold."

"Yeah, son ...I'm ...heading back ...pretty... soon," he answered, his voice faltering a bit as he sought air.

Brad's dad was slowing, and for a minute Brad worried that something was wrong. But he saw his dad wave and smile to someone, and he finally realized where they were.

27

There stood Mrs. Chestler on the sidewalk in front of her house. She wore a long, plaid coat and a brightly colored scarf covered her head. A tired, worn broom was in her gloved hands. A big, black trash can stood next to her, somehow looking irritated to be there.

His dad moved forward, wrapping one arm around Mrs. Chestler's small shoulder. She looked up at him, smiling. Her lips moved, but no sound reached Brad. He stood frozen, straddling his bike.

Brad scanned the yard. Leaves were scattered about, with a few in small piles here and there. Jagged chunks of orange littered the sidewalk. As Brad stared at the mess, the pieces of the broken jack-o-lantern stared accusingly back at him.

He glanced back at his dad, but his eyes couldn't remain there. He slowly followed the line of light poles as they curved toward the house. Reluctantly, he looked toward the porch. The last pole leaned crazily, the shattered fixture at the top bent and ruined. Wires streamed from the pole. It became a scarecrow, and Brad realized it was scaring him away from this house.

But his dad had other ideas, and he motioned for Brad to join him as he began picking up pieces of pumpkin and tossing them into the trash can.

CHAPTER 5
SATURDAY, NOVEMBER 1
AFTERNOON

"Hellllooooo!"

"Hi, Mrs. Castillo? This is Brad. Is Rudy home?"

"Oh, hello, my darling Brad! How are you doing, you delightful child?"

"Ahhhh, pretty well, Mrs. Castillo. How are you?"

"Oh, how sweet! You asked about me. None of Brad's other friends ever ask about me!"

"Umm, you're welcome."

"Oh, Brad, I am doing so well--now that you asked. You have made my day!"

"That's good...I'm glad. That's, um.... that's really great.... Mrs. Castillo?"

"Yes, beautiful boy?"

"Is, ah... is Rudy there?"

"Oh, yes, yes, yes...I am so ridiculous!"

Brad shook his head a little, then laughed at Rudy's mom. He could hear her calling loudly for Rudy. Brad waited several minutes, and was about to hang up, when he finally heard Rudy's somewhat disinterested voice.

"Hey, what's up?"

"Hey, Rudy. My mom said you called this morning."

"Yeah, like about eight hours ago."

"Get real," Brad said with a chuckle. "You didn't call me at 6:00 in the morning."

"I know, Ratman. I said I called at 8:00."

"You *said* you called eight hours ago, and it's 2:00 now, so that would make it..."

"Yeah, yeah, yeah, I know. So, why'd you wait 'till now to call me back, Ratman?"

"Don't call me 'Ratman'".

"Fine. Why'd you wait to call me 'till now? What if I was worried about you?"

"Sorry," Brad mumbled. "I had stuff to do."

"You had so much stuff you couldn't make one phone call?"

"I wasn't near a phone."

"What, was you off fishing?" Rudy asked sarcastically.

"*Were* you fishing," Brad corrected.

"No, I wasn't fishing, I was worried my, my...sup... supposedly friend was hurt or something!"

"I meant you should say, 'Were you fishing?' not '*Was* you fishing?'"

"Were you?"

"No, no. I wasn't fishing." Brad paused a moment, then asked, "Rudy, were you..."

Rudy interrupted him, "I told you I was not fishing either!"

Brad sighed deeply, then asked again, "Rudy, I meant were you worried?"

"Heck yeah, I was worried!" Rudy's voice rose, "We turn around and- poof- you're gone like you're Hondini or something."

"Houdini."

"Who what?" Rudy asked.

"Never mind. Rudy, listen: I wasn't exactly having what you'd call a great time last night, and I don't think you were either."

"So?"

"So, I was sick of Arnie and Curt, and I couldn't stand being around 'em anymore."

"So, you take off like a chicken and leave us wondering if you got hit by a car or something?" Rudy asked, his voice rising again.

Brad thought back a moment and, with a rush of guilt sweeping over him, remembered the car narrowly missing him.

"You heard that car screeching its brakes?"

"Heck yeah we heard it! We thought it nailed you, man!"

Brad stayed quiet several moments. The image of Curt dropping that pumpkin flashed in his head. He again felt the hot mixture of emotions going through him.

He spewed harshly into the phone, "Those two idiots were worse than ever! They were just Derek and Sweet wannabees!"

"And...?"

"He threw her pumpkin, Rudy!" Brad said loudly, as if that explained it all.

It was now Rudy's turn to be quiet.

Brad forced himself to imagine what it must have been like for Rudy last night. He blinked his eyes, then looked out the window at the rain that had begun to fall. He saw that it even had some wet snow mixed in it.

He swallowed, then said quietly, "I'm sorry, Rudy. I, um, I didn't think about you. I just, you know, just reacted."

"Overreacted."

Brad was startled by the response.

"I don't know," he answered.

"I do. You freaked, Brad, completely freaked."

Brad fought the defensiveness he felt building inside of him.

"Whatever," he said softly.

Brad figured the conversation was over and was about to tell Rudy goodbye, when he heard, "So where were you all day where you couldn't get a phone?"

"I was freezing my rear end off raking up leaves and cleaning up hunks of pumpkin," Brad answered excitedly. "And glass. I picked up broken glass," he added.

"Oh man! Your lights got busted, too?"

"No, they're fine."

"What? So, where were you?"

"Mrs. Chestler's," Brad responded.

"What! How'd you get there? You went and told her?"

"Relax. We just ended up there."

"Who is 'we'?" Rudy asked worriedly.

"My dad and me. He was running and I..."

"Your dad?! You told your dad?! Oh man, now my old man will find out since you told and..."

"Told him what, Rudy?"

"You told him that we broke that old lady's light!"

"No, I didn't. Besides *we* didn't break it, Rudy. Mr. Wannabee Curt did."

"My dad knows her. She shops at his store!" Rudy practically wailed, ignoring what Brad had said.

"Rudy, I didn't tell my dad that Curt broke it," Brad repeated.

Rudy paused, then asked, "So, why'd you have to clean it up?"

Brad stopped for a moment and thought about the question. "I told you. We just ended up there."

"Your dad help you?"

"No."

"How come?"

"Mrs. Chestler chased him home because he was all sweaty. She said something about catching his death of cold."

"He knows," Rudy said.

"Nah, he doesn't," Brad said. But inside he began to wonder.

CHAPTER 6
SUNDAY, NOVEMBER 2
MORNING

On Sunday morning, Brad slumped in the pew a little. As usual, he had started out trying to pay attention to the whole sermon. There was a gnawing in his stomach that told him he should concentrate even harder this time. But also, as usual, about 10 minutes into it, he lost what Pastor Jensen was saying. Brad noticed how the tree branches that could barely be seen behind the stained glass now had no leaves. He pictured the snow that fell into the night, blowing sporadically, when suddenly he heard Pastor Jensen's voice rise dramatically.

Brad turned his eyes back toward the pulpit. Pastor Jensen paused, then said quietly, "I'm going to repeat that." Like he did almost every week, he walked down from the pulpit and stood in the front between the first two pews.

Dramatically Pastor Jensen declared, "For the wrath of God..." and Brad immediately looked away because he always thought "wrath" sounded so mean. But he couldn't help hearing the last words that Pastor Jensen boomed, "... men who suppress the truth in unrighteousness!"

Brad didn't hear another word during the rest of the sermon. Suppress the truth, he thought. Suppress the truth. He remembered having the word "suppress" as a vocabulary word in school. Brad thought he even remembered the teacher's sentence, "The British troops tried to suppress the rebel uprising," or something like that. He could picture rebel soldiers, all in mismatched outfits, being forced backwards by a powerful army, all of them in matching uniforms. But how are you supposed to fight back truth? Brad thought. And why would that make God so mad he wanted to give you wrath- whatever that was.

During Sunday School class following the service, Brad always hoped that the leader, Pastor Dan, asked questions about the beginning of the sermon. It wasn't like Brad was the only one who didn't know the answers. It was just that he liked Pastor Dan, and he felt bad that the youth pastor was always having to answer his own questions.

After the service, Brad thought about pretending his little sore throat was a big sore throat, so he could use that as an excuse to miss Sunday School. One look at his dad discouraged that. His dad wasn't looking mean- or full of wrath. It was just that his head was tilted a little, and he was looking at Brad like he wanted to ask him a bunch of questions. Brad just waved and headed down the hall.

When he got to their class room, Nathan Fenton was the only one seated. He frantically waved to Brad, who hesitated, then moved to the seat next to Nathan.

"This is the earliest we've had snow in seven years," Nathan said before Brad was even seated.

"But there's not even any snow left on the ground," Brad responded.

"True. But there was a quarter inch of accumulation yesterday."

"Oh," Brad said, "that's good." He fidgeted a little as Nathan looked right at him. "Yeah, that's good... -- I guess that's good, isn't it?" Brad added quickly.

Nathan continued to just look at him until Pastor Dan called the rest of the kids in to sit down. Brad was busy studying his shoe tops, trying to avoid Nathan's awkward stare. He didn't notice Ashley Sherman sit down in the chair to his left until she whispered hello.

After a prayer, Pastor Dan started this class as he often did by having everyone give their "temperature" for how they each felt. Brad usually gave his temperature as a seven, neither too low nor too high to attract much attention to himself. Pastor Dan started by saying he was a nine. He began explaining all the different reasons, but Brad really didn't hear. Brad really didn't listen as they went around the circle either. He kept looking at the tops of his shoes.

When it was Ashley's turn, though, Brad sat up alertly and began to blush as she all but sang out that she was feeling like a ten. He just knew she'd say some completely embarrassing comment about sitting next to him. Instead she just explained how she was thankful that she'd made some new friends at the other church's party on Halloween night. She said a few other reasons for her great mood, but Brad found himself dwelling on the idea of her having made new friends.

It stayed quiet for quite a while after Ashley was done. Brad was lost in his thoughts and didn't realize it was his turn.

Finally, Pastor Dan spoke up and asked, "Do you want to pass, Brad?"

For the second time in a few minutes, Brad again blushed. This was much hotter than before, though, because Brad realized the whole group of 14 people was staring at him. Without thinking, Brad blurted out, "Four and a half."

Pastor Dan cleared his throat and remarked, "That's a pretty low temperature, Brad. Do you want to tell us why?"

Brad stared at Pastor Dan without really seeing him. He tried to list the reasons in his head for saying four and a half. He felt some vague sort of jealousy about Ashley's comment about the party. He knew Nathan was giving him the creeps. He still felt a bunch of feelings about Halloween night. But Brad surprised himself more than anyone else when he spoke up loudly and said, "Suppress the truth!"

CHAPTER 7
SUNDAY, NOVEMBER 2
NOON

On the way home from church, Brad was glad, for once, that Frannie was whining again about Jim Oglebee. Anything to keep the attention away from him was fine, Brad thought.

"I am sooo sick of that guy! He thinks he is like a model or something, and somewhere, somehow, he now has the idea that he has a brain!" Frannie wailed.

Their mom said soothingly, "Frannie, honey, we're just leaving church."

"Yeah? So what?" Frannie roared, much louder than was necessary for being in a car.

Almost as loudly, their father shot back, "Your mother means that you're supposed to..."

"What I mean," said their mother, gently putting her hand on her husband's shoulder as she turned to face Frannie, "is that it would be nice to have pleasant things said about others, especially since we've just been worshiping and..."

"That creep worships himself!" Frannie interrupted.

"Frances Marie!" proclaimed her mother.

"I am serious! He was like combing his hair in the reflection of that picture of Jesus in the hall!" Frannie barely caught her breath as she continued, "And he's always like parading in last to Senior High Group so everyone can go like, 'Ooooh, here comes Jim. Ooooh, he's so fine!'"

Mr. Bateman laughed, to Brad's surprise, and said, "You sure seem to spend a lot of time watching him."

Even louder than before, Frannie yelled, "Oh, pah-leez!!!!
Give me a break! Don't *even* think I have anything but, like,
contempt for that guy!"

"Contempt? Wow, that Honors English class is really
making a difference," Mr. Bateman chuckled. "So why the
comment about him thinking 'he has a brain'?"

"I don't want to talk about him," Frannie said, crossing her
arms and looking out the window.

"I can't believe he started, like, going off about *truth* - like
he doesn't like, like lie about stuff all the time!" Frannie continued.
"I mean he was all quoting Pastor Jensen and everything, like he
was like actually listening or something."

Nobody else said anything. Brad began to fidget a little and
was glad they were turning onto Hampshire. As they pulled into
the garage, Brad quickly unbuckled and started to open the door.

He stopped, though, when he heard his dad ask, "Were you
listening today, Brad?"

Brad waited until Frannie and his mom went inside, then he
answered, "Yeah, Dad, pretty much."

"So, what'd you think, son?"

"About what?"

"About what you heard this morning, Brad. Don't play
games," his father said, a trace of irritation in his voice.

"Ummm, well, I really didn't get the part about wrath. I
mean isn't that sort of like being mean to someone?"

"Mean? If getting punishment for something you did wrong
is mean, then I suppose so. But I don't think that's the point."

He waited a minute, and Brad said nothing.

Stroking his beard, his father asked, "What else did you
hear, Brad?"

In a quiet voice, and without looking up, Brad responded,
"Something about, um, suppressing the truth or something."

"Oh." His dad sat, just looking at him a minute.

Brad began to feel even more uncomfortable. He didn't
know what to say or do. His dad obviously knew that they broke
Mrs. Chestler's light. But he hadn't told that part of the story to

37

his mom and dad. He thought about the panic in Rudy's voice on the phone. He didn't want to get the guys in trouble.

"What does that mean to you?" his dad said suddenly, startling Brad.

He knew his dad would be mad if he asked what he meant, so Brad waited a moment, thinking of his answer.

Looking up, but not at his dad, Brad said, "I guess that if you, um, don't tell everything about something, then it's sort of like lying."

"Huh," his dad replied, again rubbing the whiskers on his chin. He looked out the window, away from Brad, and seemed about to say something.

Brad looked at him, not sure what his dad would say. He said nothing for a moment, just kept looking out the window. Brad started composing excuses in his mind for why he never said anything about the broken light. He didn't have a good one yet, when his dad turned toward him.

Brad swallowed.

His dad cleared his throat. Then he rubbed his beard yet again.

He turned in his seat to look Brad in the eyes. Brad glanced up at him, then quickly back down again.

"Brad?"

"Um, yeah, Dad?" he said, again looking up, then down hastily.

"You ready to go watch the Broncos game?"

Brad sat up in his seat, cleared his throat, then began, "Well, Dad, the thing is that we, um.... Broncos? Go watch the Broncos?"

"Yes, Brad. You remember them?"

"Yeah, yeah...Oh yeah, I do. Yeah, let's go... let's go watch 'em."

As his dad got out of the car, Brad exhaled. He exhaled again, before getting out and following his father into the house.

CHAPTER 8
MONDAY, NOVEMBER 3
MORNING

On Monday morning Brad's clock radio went off at 6:30. The song that was playing mixed awkwardly with his dream. Brad automatically rolled over, hoping to get back to the pleasant dream he was having. But the song kept playing, and Brad slowly awakened to the idea that he needed to get up and get going. He rolled onto his back and let out a deep breath, as he folded his hands behind his head. He looked at the ceiling, focusing on the designs formed there, and wondering if he could again spot the one that looked like a whale.

Before he could find that design, the song ended and the irritating voice of the over-caffeinated D.J. slammed into Brad's ears. He reached over and shut the clock off. He pulled himself out of bed and headed down the hall to the bathroom. Before he even reached the door, Frannie yelled from inside the bathroom, "Go away, Brad! I've still got 10 minutes, you loser."

Brad grunted and shuffled down the stairs. His mom came bounding up the stairs, smiling like she'd won the lottery. She handed Brad the cordless phone, and sang out, "Good morning, honey! It's Rudy!"

Brad took the phone and sat down on the step, as his mom bounced back down.

"Hey..." he mumbled.

"What's up?" Rudy asked.

"Nothing... I'm trying to wake up."

"Hey, you want a ride to school? My mom's got to take my sister in 'cuz she's got this big old honking project."

"Yeah, sure... Will there be room for me?"

"The project's not that big, dude!" Rudy laughed.

Brad chuckled a minute and realized he hadn't heard Rudy laugh like that for a long time.

"O.K., so we'll be over there in like 20 minutes or something."

"Really? That soon?" Brad asked.

"I don't know- maybe half an hour or so. Just be ready."

"O.K. Later."

"Later," Rudy said.

Just as Brad was putting toothpaste on his brush, Frannie hollered up the stairs, "Your little friend Rudolph is here." Brad shoved the toothbrush in his mouth and brushed quickly three times on each side. As he rinsed his mouth, he looked in the mirror and groaned at his hair. He pulled the hairbrush through it one time, not making a bit of difference. He grabbed his backpack from his room and raced down the stairs.

At the front door, he called out, "Bye!"

His dad called out a goodbye and his mom yelled, "Wait, honey, your lunch!"

Brad yelled back, "It's Subway on Mondays, I'll just buy lunch!" But as he was finishing, his mom was already there holding his lunch bag and reaching out her arms. Brad hugged her, grabbed the bag, and went out the door.

"Thanks- love you!" he called, as he ran down the sidewalk.

As he climbed into the Castillo's van, Rudy's mom said, "Oh, Brad Sweet Boy, you told your mommy you love her! You are just too precious, you angel child!" She was turned around looking back at Brad, smiling her huge smile. Brad felt his familiar blushing and didn't know what to do or say. She kept smiling at him, and he was about to say something when Rudy said, "Mom, do you want us to be late, or what?"

Brad was relieved when Rudy's mom and his sister, Marissa, immediately started talking back and forth excitedly as she pulled the van out into the street. He glanced over at Rudy, who just rolled his eyes and shook his head.

After helping Rudy and Marissa deliver the project to the science lab, Brad glanced at his watch.

"Thanks for the ride. I've got to quick get my math book from my locker," Brad said, as he turned out of the doorway into the hall- and a sea of people. It didn't matter what time of day it was, it always seemed to Brad like he was going the wrong way in the hall. Dodging people all headed the other direction, Brad made his way to his locker. He had three minutes to get his book and on to math. As he turned the corner, he heard a loud, familiar voice.

There was Arnie, whose locker was two away from Brad's, telling the four kids standing near him, "...and then Curt like slam dunked this pumpkin down on this old lady's light fixture, and, man, that thing like...EXPLODED!"

The boys who were listening responded with the expected "Awesome!" and "Cool!" comments that fed Arnie's ego. Brad slid behind them, and with his back to the group, urgently twisted 12-24-7 on his locker. As the door popped open, he grabbed the book, shut the door, started to leave, then heard, "...and that wussy Ratman ran away! He took off running and crying like a kindygardner!"

Brad stopped where he was, thought about continuing to class, then he turned. Arnie was laughing like crazy, and the other boys were, too. Arnie looked over another boy's shoulder and stopped laughing when he saw Brad. He started to say something, but the warning bell sounded.

The other boys noticed Brad, and a couple of them slipped away. Two of them stayed, and the taller one, who looked kind of familiar, said, "Is this the wussy kindygardner you were talking about, Arnie?" Arnie looked at Brad, then at the other boy. Brad stared at Arnie, who cleared his throat. With a smirk on his face, the taller boy said, "This is the one, ain't it, Arnie?" Arnie again looked at that boy, then back to the other boy on his right side. Finally, he said, "Yeah, that's Brad."

"The wussy?" asked the boy on the right, looking right at Brad.

Arnie looked fleetingly at Brad, then away, and said, "Yeah, the wussy."

The tall boy patted Arnie on the back and laughed. The three of them walked down the hall, Arnie in the middle.

Brad stood staring, his math book in one hand, his backpack in the other. Arnie said something he couldn't hear, and the others again laughed. Brad felt heat climbing down his neck, and he started toward Arnie. The tardy bell screamed loudly in his ear, and Brad stopped. He felt so mad at that jerk Arnie. He took one more step toward him, then turned and ran the other way down the hall toward math class.

CHAPTER 9
MONDAY, NOVEMBER 3
LUNCH TIME

After science, Brad automatically headed for his locker to get his lunch. As he turned the corner and saw his locker, he immediately flashed back to before school and Arnie. Anger again rose up in him. Brad did not want to go to the cafeteria and deal with him. Who knew how many more times Arnie had told his thrilling story? He peeked through the doorway of the nearby class and was relieved to see sun shining through the window. He turned around to head outside when he saw Arnie, Curt, and the tall boy who was with Arnie that morning walking toward him. It was too late to do anything else, so he stood waiting for them, groaning.

"Hey, Sutter, there's your wuss buddy!" the tall boy yelled, causing a few people in the hall to laugh.

As they neared, Arnie sang out, "Yo, what's up, Brat?" He was beaming like he'd hit a home run.

Brad thought for a split second about just leaving, then the look on Arnie's face got to him. Seeing Arnie's chubby cheeks sitting on top of his phony smile was too much.

"What's up is the vomit in my throat," Brad said icily.

"Cool!" Arnie laughed. "You gonna puke?"

"If I do, it will be on you," Brad shot back, and regretted it as soon as he said it.

"Whoa, check out Mr. Bad!" the tall boy said.

Brad shook his head, wishing he'd kept his mouth shut.

"You gonna take that, Sutter?" goaded the tall boy.

"Yeah," Arnie said, trying to put his mean look on his face.

"You are?" Curt asked.

"I mean no," Arnie said, his eyes closing even tighter. Obviously not sure what the tall boy was expecting him to do, Arnie crossed his arms over his chest and shifted from foot to foot, waiting for a clue.

Curt spoke up and said, "What's your problem, Brat Ratman?"

Jumping on Curt's assist, Arnie said, "Yeah, Brat, what's your deal?" Brad noticed Arnie glance at the tall boy. Always looking for approval, Brad thought.

Several things raced through Brad's mind. He consciously tried to smother the rage that was inside him. He saw the tall boy nudge Arnie. Again not sure what to do, Arnie repeated, "So what's your problem, Brat Ratman?"

Brad was furious. He knew he was turning red; he knew he was about to boil over. He hated that Arnie was winning his stupid game by making him this livid. It didn't help, either, that five or six other people had gathered around by then.

Still, everything he wanted to say would have made things worse. Brad hurriedly started to move down the hall, not even sure where he was going. He vaguely heard the tall kid saying something, but he just kept going.

Suddenly Arnie said loudly, "So, Wuss Man, which girlfriend you going to go see- Ashley or Mrs. Chestler?"

Brad reacted instantly. He spun around so fast, his backpack smacked him in the side of the face. Everyone started laughing, and Brad thought he was going to lose what was left of his sanity. He looked at the crowd of laughing faces, and the sound was deafening to him. He thought he was going to explode.

He felt that burning in his eyes, and he told himself he absolutely would not allow himself to let even one drop of a tear fall. He tightened his face to force the tears back. A hundred things flew in his mind to scream out to Arnie. He squeezed his face so hard, he began to tremble slightly.

The group continued to laugh, and Brad just ran. He ran as fast as he could down the hall. He bumped into one girl and stopped momentarily to apologize. His backpack hit a boy as he turned the corner, and the boy hollered, "Jerk!" but Brad kept going.

He ran to the outside doors and shoved them open. He ran past the bike rack and toward the trees near the track. He no longer ran but walked urgently. Nearing the same tree under which he sat the other day while his dad ran, Brad hurled his backpack at the oak. It hit it straight on, then dropped, looking like a wounded bird as it fell to the ground.

Brad felt like doing the same thing to Arnie. Or to Curt. Or to himself.

Instead, he plopped down against the tree, on the side opposite the school. He let his head drop; his chin rested on his chest. Brad sat, thinking nothing, just letting the wrath escape from him.

CHAPTER 10
MONDAY, NOVEMBER 3
AFTER SCHOOL

For the second school day in a row, Brad walked toward the bathroom after his last class. Unlike on Halloween, though, he wasn't sure if the guys would be looking for him. He still was surprised that neither Curt nor Arnie had said anything to him in English class after lunch. He'd walked in at the same time as Rudy, who thankfully didn't seem to know anything about the big hallway episode-- yet. Arnie and Curt came in tardy, as usual. They didn't seem to act any differently. They did their normal throwing of eraser pieces around the room when Mrs. Seversen wasn't looking. They drew their normal grotesque pictures of people picking their noses. They did nothing they didn't always do. Which made Brad nervous.

So, he had gone into the bathroom again hoping to avoid them. He was surprised by the number of boys in there when he walked in. He thought about turning around, but he had enough attention drawn to him for one day without looking like a geek who couldn't handle a crowd. He saw one door to a stall that wasn't fully shut, so he pushed it open. Sitting on the toilet was an 8th grader. Brad gasped, and the older boy gave a look like a bull charging a matador. Brad mumbled, "Oops," and pulled the door shut. The door of the last stall opened, and Brad was almost afraid to look, considering how things were going. But it was another boy Brad didn't know. He waited for the boy to pass, then Brad slipped into that stall. He made sure to lock the door.

He sat down without looking, and almost fell in; the last boy obviously hadn't needed the seat down. Brad hung his backpack on the door hook and decided just to stand. His stomach growled. Brad thought that was a bit disgusting, given where he was. But he remembered he hadn't eaten lunch. He looked in the sack his mom had packed. The sandwich was a smashed pile of goo. The chips were crumbled beyond hope. What were once apparently Oreos now was a fine black and white powder. Brad grabbed the apple. It had a few bruises, but he took a huge bite anyway.

He stood eating his apple, not really paying any attention to the various conversations outside his stall. He did wonder why so many middle school boys had to cuss so much. He guessed it made them feel tougher. It just sounded stupid to Brad. As he finished his apple, and was wondering where to put the core, he realized it was quiet. He looked at his watch, which read 3:14. Surely those guys would be gone 14 minutes after school was out. He grabbed his pack and opened the stall door. One boy was just leaving the bathroom, and as the door opened, Brad heard a familiar yell from down the hall, "Wait a minute, dudes, nature's calling!"

Brad dropped his backpack on the middle of the floor, crossed his arms, and sighed. No escaping him now. Arnie burst into the bathroom, already loosening his belt. Seeing Brad, he stopped in the doorway.

"Hey, Brad. What's up.... I mean, um, h-h-how's it going?" Arnie stuttered.

Brad stared at Arnie, but said nothing.

Suddenly Arnie stuck out his arm, and Brad jumped back.

"No, sorry, I'm, um, I'm like trying to shake, you know, like telling you I'm... you know. Here," Arnie said, again putting his hand out toward Brad.

Brad stayed where he was.

"Brad, I'm like sorry, man," Arnie said, his hand still outstretched.

"You are sorry," Brad said, his hands now in his pockets.

Arnie smiled a little, then said, "Yeah, so great, so everything's cool between us and all." He began bouncing a little from side to side. "So, we're all like cool and all and everything---and I really gotta go!" Arnie stated loudly, rushing into the nearest stall.

Brad stood a moment, wondering what just happened. Did Arnie really think that things were all right between them, that his attempt at an apology really put their friendship back where it once was? "He's even more stupid than I thought," Brad mumbled quietly, as he picked up his backpack.

Judging from the sounds in the stall, Arnie wasn't lying about needing to go. Brad knew it was time for him to go, too, so he slung his backpack over his shoulder and left.

CHAPTER 11
TUESDAY, NOVEMBER 4
LUNCH TIME

As he walked into the cafeteria, Brad chuckled. Mr. Pierson, the 6th grade counselor, walked by with his 80's style hair, long in the back, and his earring. Brad thought of the movie he'd seen the night before. He hadn't put it together then, but Brad realized how Mr. Pierson was a lot like the main character in the movie. He tried so hard to be cool, but just made a fool of himself instead. For a moment, Brad thought about asking Mr. Pierson if he'd seen the movie *Cool Man*. But when Brad turned back to him, he was walking into the main office. Brad smiled at himself, knowing that he'd never really ask him anyway.

Brad couldn't remember the last time the four people in his family had gone to a movie together. He was so glad they had done it last night. It was sure a nice change from the way things had been going. Frannie had tried all kinds of ways to get out of it, but even she was laughing crazily during the film.

The morning had gone O.K. so far. He'd left on his bike before anyone could stop by his house to walk with him. He understood the math they had done. In music class Rudy sat between Curt and him. Curt had leaned over Rudy, raised his eyebrows, and started to say something to Brad when Mr. Leinenger loudly said, "People, we have a double ton of work to do today, so listen up!"

Mr. Leinenger kept them so busy introducing all the songs they had to learn for the Christmas concert that the only thing Curt had time to say was, "Christmas already? Jeesh, that's like a million miles from now!"

Brad had managed to leave the music room quickly and slipped into geography before Curt did. They had assigned seats there and Ms. Cruz must have known what she was doing because the four boys were in four different corners of the room. Curt was across from Brad, and he was trying to mouth something to Brad. He didn't try very hard to figure out what Curt was saying. Ms. Cruz told Curt to pay attention, and several kids near him chuckled. Brad was relieved when the whole class read out of the textbook. It was boring, but at least he didn't have to do a small group assignment. Curt always managed to get into Brad's group and expected him to do all the work. His next class, science, was actually good. Neither Curt, Rudy, nor Arnie was in his class, and for once Brad liked the experiment they had done.

So, Brad was in a good mood as he strolled into the cafeteria. He didn't think about where to go, he just automatically headed toward the table where he always sat. There was the usual raucous noise in there. Girls were scurrying from one table to the next, getting the latest gossip on which boy was "going" with which girl. Boys were wolfing their food down, then trying to figure out how to get more to eat.

Rudy sat down right after Brad had taken a bite of his sandwich. He asked Brad, "Can you even believe what those two did?"

Brad started to talk, but his mouth was full. He chewed twice, swallowed, and instantly regretted not taking more time because of the pain in his throat the large bite caused. He drank a quick gulp from his juice carton.

Brad quickly asked, "Who did what?"

Rudy answered, "Oh man, you didn't see it? How could you miss it, man, it's right out front!"

Brad thought for a moment, trying to figure out what he missed in front of the school that could be so obvious. It dawned on him that he had come into school from the back entrance because he'd locked his bike in the rack.

"I didn't come in that way," Brad explained. "So, what did Curt and Arnie do?" Brad asked, thinking that this was what Curt had been so anxious to tell him.

"Curt and Arnie did some, too?" Rudy asked incredulously. "Oh, man, I didn't know that!" he exclaimed. "Wow! Curt and Arnie? I can't believe those guys," Rudy continued, a trace of admiration in his voice.

"Curt and Arnie did *what*?" Brad asked. "I don't even know what you're talking about!"

Just then the unmistakable voice of Arnie bellowed, "Hello, ladies!"

Brad looked up to see Arnie, Curt, and the tall boy who was with Arnie the day before all sitting down next to them.

"I can't believe you guys did some, too!" Rudy yelled excitedly.

Arnie's round cheeks instantly sagged from a big grin into a grimace. Shooting a look at Mr. Andrews, the assistant principal, Arnie then turned to Rudy. He pointed his index finger at Rudy's nose and tersely spoke, "Number one, shut up. Number two, what the heck are you talking about?"

Rudy looked nervously around. He almost whispered, "He just told me that you guys did some, too."

"Who did?" Arnie asked, again glancing at Mr. Andrews.

"You and Curt!" Rudy declared.

"No, you idiot! Who lied about me and Curt?"

"Brad told me-- just a minute ago," Rudy answered loudly, his voice cracking.

Brad laughed weakly and said, "I seriously do not even have a clue what we're talking about." He looked around at the four pairs of eyes staring directly at his. "What I *asked* Rudy was what you two supposedly did...because I do not have one single idea what is going on!" Brad said, his voice rising as he finished.

Arnie looked at Brad with a slight smirk. "Come on, Ratma...Bateman. What else would we be talking about? The only thing everyone else is talking about!"

Brad stuttered, "Th..th... the only thing I do know is that whatever this big deal is must have happened in front of the school," he stopped to catch his breath and pointed to Rudy, "...and as I told Mr. Rude Man here, I haven't even been to the front of the school today because I rode my bike!" He took a deep breath and exhaled.

Curt spoke up and accusingly demanded, "Yeah? Show us your bike key then, Brat!"

Brad stared at Curt, thinking he looked especially rodent-like just then, and reached into his collar and pulled out the chain that held his key.

Curt stared open-mouthed, but said nothing.

Arnie chuckled and asked, "You really *don't* know what's going on?"

"I don't," Brad simply said.

Rudy spoke up and eagerly said, "You didn't see the graffiti that Derek and Sweet did?"

Arnie joined in, leaning forward and saying conspiratorially, "You gotta see it! They dissed this school and a whole bunch of the teachers. Dude, you'd think these guys are like professionals or something. I mean, it's like art or something!"

Curt now beamed with pride. He nodded his head smugly and said, "Those guys are good, I mean *really* good."

The tall kid added, "I'm telling you, my cousin is phat."

Brad looked at him, confused. Cousin? One of those guys is his cousin?

Arnie said, "I bet you can't wait to see it now, huh, Brad?"

Brad nodded, then when he realized they were expecting an answer, he said, "Yeah, um, really... I've got to see that..."

Caught up in the growing excitement, Rudy all but hollered, "Man, they should give tagging lessons or something!"

This time Curt turned to look at Mr. Andrews before crisply saying, "Rudy, would you shut your trap? You're going to get my brother in trouble!"

Everyone grew quiet then. Mr. Andrews looked up from the group of students with whom he was talking. He started toward the doors out to the office, then turned suddenly and walked straight toward their table.

Folding his hands over his mouth, Arnie muttered, "Cool, Rudy! If they're busted, then you're dead meat!"

Despite his brown skin, Rudy turned noticeably red.

"Hi, fellas!" Mr. Andrews greeted in his always-too-loud voice, as he stood right behind Arnie.

All five boys said some variation of hello, trying to appear calm.

"Well, fellas, as you probably know, some individuals decided to desecrate our lovely school with spray paint," Mr. Andrews boomed.

Arnie spoke with faked sincerity, "Really, sir? I don't believe we were aware of that terrible news. Why would anyone mark up the front of Kingston?"

Mr. Andrews put his hands on Arnie's shoulders and replied, "Arnie, why would anyone who claims to know nothing about this ask me about paint in the front of the school, when I said nothing about where it was?"

Brad heard Curt mumble, "Because he's got no brain!"

"What's that, Curt?" Mr. Andrews asked, still with his hands on Arnie's shoulders.

Curt looked up, and with his voice even higher than normal, said, "I just said whoever did that has no brains. I think it was really stupid, Mr. Andrews."

"I do, too, Mr. Compton," Mr. Andrews answered. Looking at each of the boys, he continued, "I'm pretty sure you boys saw that mess this morning before it got sandblasted off- especially you, Sutter," his hands gripping Arnie's shoulders even tighter. "We'll find out who the losers are who did this, and they will pay." He paused a moment, letting the words sink in. "It would sure be nice to get some information that any of you fellas has about this." He stood a moment longer, a slight grin on his face. "Have a good day, gentlemen!" he roared as he turned and began to walk away.

Just as Arnie was opening his mouth, Mr. Andrews pivoted back to them and said, "Oh, I forgot to tell you something." He slid two steps closer. "Just spread the word that if anyone does know anything about this but doesn't tell me--they'll be facing stiff consequences, too." Once more he loudly said, "Have a good day, fellas!" as he moved off toward the door.

Nobody said anything this time.

Brad looked up and again felt four pairs of eyes drilling into him.

"What?!" he asked, raising his hands palms upward.

Arnie looked at him, as seriously as Arnie could, and said, "You just better keep your mouth shut, Brad. If you say anything--anything! -- you'll be in a whole lot more trouble than Old Man Andrews can dish out..."

CHAPTER 12
WEDNESDAY, NOVEMBER 5
DINNER TIME

"Brad, you're just playing with your dinner. You've always liked my spaghetti, Sweetie," chirped Mrs. Bateman. "What's the problem?"

"Oh, nothing, Mom," Brad responded. "I guess I'm just tired or something."

"Well, you better eat up, son," Brad's dad stated. "We've got to leave to youth group in about half an hour."

With his elbow on the table, Brad rested his forehead on his palm. "Youth group?!" he thought. "Oh, brother!" He hadn't even thought about this being the first Wednesday in the month.

"What's the matter, honey, are you sick?" asked his mother worriedly, as she got up to feel his cheeks.

Brad thought for a moment about taking advantage of the opportunity his mom had just presented him, but then he realized he'd just have to go to bed. Instead, he said, "No, I'm fine. It's just that I've got this huge old geography test, and I was going to study for that tonight."

"Don't you want to go see Ashley?" Frannie asked teasingly, blinking her eyes and making what she thought was a cute face.

Both of Brad's parents stopped eating and looked at Brad.

"Is there something you want to tell us, Brad?" his mom sang, smiling ear to ear.

Brad gave Frannie a hideous grimace, and then said flatly, "Trust me, Mom, there is absolutely nothing I need to tell you about Ashley Sherman."

"Really?" asked Frannie, clearly enjoying watching Brad squirm.

"Really," he said, starting to get up from his seat.

"That's not what I've heard..." she retorted.

"Oh?" asked their dad.

"Yes, I've heard from quality sources that there's, like, some special vibes between these two!" Frannie said happily, pulling her feet up to the seat.

Brad started to pick up his plate, then suddenly had an inspiration.

"I wonder if it's the same 'quality sources' who I heard talking about you and Jim Oglebee?" he asked, tilting his head sideways, with fake curiosity.

"Now this is getting interesting!" laughed their dad.

"Come on, Dad, I told you the other day there is, like, *nothing* between Jim and me," Frannie said, trying to act nonchalant.

Brad couldn't resist. "That's what I heard- when you guys were hugging in the hall there was *nothing* between you, not even a notebook!"

"Now that is a lie!" Frannie declared emphatically. "I was like holding up my math book between us." Suddenly she wrapped her hand around her mouth, realizing what she had revealed.

"Frannie!" exclaimed their mom, her eyes popping wide.

"Frances Marie!" blurted out their dad, trying to conceal his grin.

"Whoa..." said Brad, laughing at his amazing luck in blindly guessing right.

"Ahhhhhhhhhh!!!!" screamed Frannie, as she bounded out of the kitchen.

CHAPTER 13
MONDAY, NOVEMBER 5
EVENING

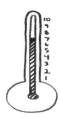

"Seven," Brad remembered to say when Pastor Dan asked his temperature at the start of Middle School Youth Group. He had actually wanted to say nine, because he was still chuckling at how he had gotten Frannie at dinner. But Brad didn't want to have to explain why he was feeling so good. After all, Ashley Sherman was sitting a few seats away, and how could he tell the story without including the part about her?

Brad had made sure to sit several seats away from Ashley. He knew Frannie would want to get back at him, and he didn't want to give her any ammunition if she somehow found out he had sat by Ashley.

"Tonight, we're going to play a game," Pastor Dan said after the last person gave her temperature. "It's called Fib," he continued, "and even though we're in a church, it's going to be legal to stretch the truth a little."

"Why?" asked Sarah Jacobs. "I thought it wasn't O.K. to lie."

"I'm glad you're thinking," Pastor Dan responded. "And I am going to talk about that-- but not until the end." He paused a moment and looked around the circle, stopping at Brad. "Does anyone remember what the sermon was about Sunday?" he asked, continuing to look at Brad with a slight grin on his face.

"Pastor Jensen used Paul's letter to the Romans as the subject..." Nathan Fenton started, before being interrupted by Pastor Dan.

He just held his hand out to Nathan in a stop motion and was smiling at Brad as he said, "I'm pretty sure Brad remembered the most important part."

Brad started to turn red as he flashed back to blurting out "Suppress the truth!" during Sunday School. A few others recalled that, too, as chuckles and laughs bounced around the room.

"What was that famous quote, Brad?" asked Pastor Dan, as he stood up behind Brad and put his hands on his shoulders.

Brad's blushing was now in full bloom. That familiar warmth spread across to his ears. He knew his face was red, but he looked up at the ring of smiling faces and somehow could laugh at himself. After a couple of false starts that were interrupted by his own nervous laughter and the giggling of others, Brad finally belted out, "Suppress the truth!"

The others started clapping, and despite trying again to suppress his blushing, Brad once more turned crimson. Pastor Dan spoke up right away saying, "Well done, Mr. Bateman," as he patted Brad on the back. "Now, what is that supposed to mean?" he asked, quieting everyone. Brad was relieved to see that the question was directed at the group, not just him this time.

Everyone seemed to be waiting for Nathan. However, he sat still, apparently not wanting to get interrupted again.

"Come on guys. 'Suppress the truth.' What's it mean?" Pastor Dan implored. "Sarah, what about you? Tell us what you think it might mean."

"I don't know," she started. "I guess it's probably got like something to do with lying. Or at least not telling the truth."

"Okay!" Pastor Dan exclaimed. "Good! Now is telling a lie the same thing as not telling the truth?"

"Sure," said Jermaine Robinson. "It's just a different way of saying it."

"Does everyone agree with that?" asked Pastor Dan.

Most of the group members nodded heads in agreement. But Ashley Sherman spoke up quietly and said, "I don't know."

"What don't you know, Ashley?" asked Pastor Dan gently. "What keeps you from saying that lying is the same as not telling the truth?"

"Well, I mean if I say to you that I put $100 in the offering plate on Sunday, that'd be lying."

Jermaine laughed and said, "Knowing you, Ashley, you probably put in *two* hundred!"

"Thanks- I think..." Ashley said, as the others chuckled. "But making something up that just *didn't* happen is different than *not* telling you something that really did happen."

"Huh?!" questioned Sarah.

"Can you give us an example?" asked Pastor Dan.

"Well, like say I saw Jermaine here *take* money from the offering plate..." Ashley said teasingly.

"Hey!" shouted Jermaine, as everyone laughed.

Ashley continued, "... but I didn't tell you that I saw him stealing. That's different than making something up, isn't it?"

"Interesting," remarked Pastor Dan. "What do you guys think?"

Several people started talking at once, some giving their opinions and some sharing examples of different situations having to do with lying.

Brad said nothing. He just stared at Ashley, though not really looking at her. He was thinking of his own examples. Not telling his parents about Mrs. Chestler's light fixture. Saying nothing about the graffiti that Derek and Sweet had done. Even the story about Frannie hugging Jim Oglebee. But that had apparently turned out to be true.

Lost in his own thoughts, Brad didn't notice that Pastor Dan was asking him specifically about his viewpoint.

"You seem to be the only one who hasn't said anything about this, Brad. What do you think?"

Hearing his name snapped Brad out of his reverie, but he didn't really know what he was being asked. With everyone

59

looking at him, he muttered, "Yeah, well, uh….um….yeah…..What?"

Even Pastor Dan snickered at Brad's reaction. And for what felt like the tenth time of the night, Brad felt the familiar heat rising up, spreading from his ears to his cheeks as everyone continued giggling at him.

"I'm sorry for chuckling, Brad. I should have realized you were really contemplating the question," Pastor Dan said. "I shouldn't have interrupted your thinking – and I was wrong to laugh. Forgive me, please."

Pastor Dan continued looking at Brad expectantly. Brad wasn't sure what he was supposed to do. He shifted his weight on the chair, and then he looked down at the floor.

"Can you forgive me?" Pastor Dan asked gently.

Relieved to know what he was supposed to do, Brad nodded his head vigorously. As he started to again turn his head to the floor, he noticed Ashley looking at him. She smiled slightly and maintained her gaze. Brad looked down, then very briefly back at Ashley. She was still watching him, with the same closed-mouth grin.

Brad was surprised that the warmth he felt this time was not on his face but was inside.

For the rest of the discussion Brad tried to pay attention so he at least could give some reasonable answer if he was again asked to respond. Almost all the kids wanted to share about some situation he or she had been in that dealt with telling – or not telling – the truth. Brad was very relieved that no one brought up the graffiti at school. If anyone said something about it, he felt like his face would be a bright billboard telling everyone that he knew who did the vandalism.

Pastor Dan interrupted the last people who were talking over each other trying to tell their stories by saying, "Sorry to cut you off, but we're out of time."

He paused as the last stubborn voices faded.

"Before you go, I'm actually going to give you a homework assignment."

Groans and moans filled the room. Pastor Dan raised both his arms and smiled as he said, "Wait, wait, waaaait! It's not *that* big of a deal, people!"

He hesitated while the whining ended and said, "I just want each of you to find some time before our next meeting next month to talk with your parents about this topic. Who knows – maybe Mom or Dad will tell you about a time when *they* didn't tell the truth. Imagine that!"

That brought laughter back in the room and the sounds continued out the door as the kids left for the night.

CHAPTER 14
THURSDAY, NOVEMBER 6
MORNING

Brad was twice given opportunities to get his "homework" done right away, both the night before and at breakfast that morning. First, during the car ride home his dad asked both Frannie and him the typical question regarding what they talked about in youth group. Brad didn't mind a bit when Frannie charged right in and described every detail about the high school session. He was relieved that she yapped the whole way home. Brad figured she didn't want to give him even a second to bring up Jim Oglebee.

At breakfast Brad's mom cheerfully asked, "So, dear, how was youth group last night?"

Sensing that a follow-up question was sure to come, Brad readied a huge spoonful of cereal before he quickly said, "Fine". As his mom asked the predictable question regarding what they talked about, he quickly shoved the whole spoonful into his mouth, keeping him from being able to answer right away. Frannie unwittingly bailed him out again as she came flying into the kitchen, her book-bag and purse each swinging wildly as she reached for a piece of toast and, nearly knocking over a juice glass in the process, also grabbed a banana.

"Bye! Gotta go!" Frannie hollered as she launched out the front door.

"Bye, Sweetie," Mrs. Bateman said, as she turned to look out the window at her daughter running down the sidewalk.

"That girl knows two speeds, Mach 1 and tortoise," she said, still looking out the window.

"Yeah, that's for sure," Brad said, not really knowing what was meant, but realizing the subject had been changed.

Even though he could've eaten another bowl, Brad quickly downed the rest of his cereal and brought the bowl to the sink.

"Thanks, Mom!" he hollered as he bounded up the steps.

CHAPTER 15
THURSDAY, NOVEMBER 6
AFTERNOON

As Brad walked from math class to music, he was startled by Curt, who grabbed Brad's elbow and nudged him from the main hall into the alcove of the emergency exit.

"What are you doing?" Brad managed to say.

Looking back and forth both ways down the main hall, Curt put a finger to his mouth and said, "Shhhh!"

"What are you shushing me about, Curt? I'm trying to get to class. And you're in the same class!"

"Duh. I know that, dude," Curt whispered hoarsely. "I just don't want to get busted by Leinenger."

"You are making NO sense. Busted for what?"

Again, Curt put his finger up to quiet Brad, as his eyes looked conspiratorially back and forth down the hall. After a couple moments, he patted the outside of his backpack and said, "Check it out!"

"What? It's the same backpack you've had since 4th grade."

"No, dummy, check out the inside."

"Uh, hello, I left my spyglasses at home. I can't see in there!"

"Oh never mind, dweeb. Just meet me after school by the bike racks. This is sooooo cool!"

With that, Curt took off down the hall toward the music room. With a pit in his stomach, Brad followed.

Seeing Curt practically hop down the hall in excitement reminded Brad of a time a couple of years ago. It was at Curt's birthday party and they had gone to FunLand Amusement Park. It was a big deal because Curt had never had a party there. Most of his birthdays had been in their backyard with frozen pizza and running through the sprinkler. Curt was so excited that day, mostly because the four buddies were actually at FunLand riding the rides and having a great time. He seemed to bounce from place to place, grinning the entire time. Curt especially lit up when he saw his dad coming toward them when they were in line for the roller coaster. Brad remembered then that Curt's dad never seemed to be at his other birthday parties. This time he motioned for Curt to step out of line, and when he did his dad slipped something in his hand, rubbed his head, then took off from where he had appeared. Curt stood looking at his dad as he walked away, still smiling. He ran back to Rudy, Arnie, and Brad in line and shouted, "Ice cream!" as he held open both hands to show a wrinkled wad of cash.

As the bell rang to mark the end of the last class, Brad wished he had not ridden his bike. He thought for a second about turning around to go out the front of school and walking home, pretending that he had forgotten that he had ridden. But then he looked out the window and saw Curt shifting from foot to foot like he needed to find a bathroom in a hurry, frantically waving Brad to him. With a deep exhale, Brad adjusted the backpack on his shoulder and walked out the double door.

Curt had his backpack between his feet, with the top flap pulled open. He looked around furtively, then quickly covered his pack up when a boy came up right next to them and unlocked his bike. When Brad started to ask why Curt was being so secretive, he was instantly hushed by Curt hissing, "Dude! Shut it!"

The boy took off, and for the third time that afternoon Curt practically had his head on a swivel as he apparently tried to see if anyone was watching them. Finally, he reopened the top of the pack and whispered, "Check it out!"

Brad leaned over to look in, and he was a little surprised to see two cans of spray paint. He first thought of the project that Ms. Cruz had talked about in geography class, but then realized that groups weren't yet picked. Why was Curt showing him paint he apparently was going to use for a project that wasn't even assigned yet? Just as Brad opened his mouth to ask about it, Curt practically whistled, "Is this awesome or what?!"

"I guess..." Brad muttered.

"You guess?" Curt asked, then loudly screeched, "You stinkin' guess?!"

Brad wasn't sure how to react.

"Brat – listen. We're going to use this paint tomorrow night to tag Wabash," motioning his head toward their former elementary school next door.

Brad felt like puking. He looked down and shook his head slightly from side to side.

"Do not tell me Brat Ratman doesn't think this is cool!" Curt said.

Brad looked at him. Instead of saying what he really thought, that it was stupid, dumb, idiotic and a sure way to get them into tons of trouble, he simply and weakly said, "When?"

Interpreting the question as Brad's agreement to join in, Curt excitedly said, "We're going to do it about 9:00! We're spending the night at Arnie's, then we're sneaking out and doing this thing!"

As Curt started to say something else, he was interrupted by the sound of Arnie bellowing as he came around the corner. "Think you can talk any louder, Curt? Jeesh – I could hear you walking out from M Hall!"

"Yeah, well who's the loud one now, dorkus?" Curt practically shouted.

"Shut up!" Arnie yelled, matching Curt's volume.

As the two of them continued their hollering match, Brad quickly unlocked his bike, hopped on, and rode off without saying anything.

CHAPTER 16
FRIDAY, NOVEMBER 7
MORNING

Brad was brushing his teeth with one hand and petting an appreciative Tripp with the other when he heard the phone ring. Of course, Frannie practically sprinted to answer it. Her enthusiasm quickly ebbed as she hollered out, "It's your chubster friend Arnold calling for you, loser!"

Though Brad was just about done, he continued brushing frantically and walked out into the hall, shrugging his shoulders, as if to show Frannie he couldn't possibly take a phone call now. Offering no help whatsoever, Frannie simply set the phone down and headed back to her room. Grunting in frustration, Brad stepped back into the bathroom, spat, and quickly rinsed off his toothbrush. With both hands on the sink and looking down, Brad knew Arnie was going to tell him about the sleepover. He didn't know what to do.

He stepped back into the hall and looked at the phone, the mouthpiece seemingly aimed right at him, daring Brad to pick it up. Brad stared at it, trying to think of something – *anything*- he could use as an excuse not to go to Arnie's. Suddenly, almost spastically, Brad lunged across the hall and popped the phone onto the cradle. He raced into his room, narrowly missing Tripp who was lying in the doorway, grabbed his backpack, flew down the stairs, and bellowed, "Bye, Mom and Dad!" just as the phone starting ringing again.

Throwing the front door open, Brad had to leap sideways to avoid smashing straight into Frannie's friend Tanya.

"Oops – sorry 'bout that," Brad managed as he headed hurriedly down the front sidewalk.

"Watch it, Brat!" Tanya blurted. "I do not *even* need a broken leg for our dance recital tonight!"

Dance recital. Brad stopped and smiled a moment as he said out loud, "Dance recital. Huh."

CHAPTER 17
FRIDAY, NOVEMBER 7
EVENING

Brad made a point of telling each of the guys separately during the day that he couldn't go to the sleepover at Arnie's because he had to go his sister's dance recital. He tried hard to act really disappointed each time. Rudy was the first one he told, and Brad felt a little bad that he sort of made up the part about *having* to go because his parents never actually said that he did. But he rationalized his story by telling himself he DID have to go, or he would go insane with those knuckleheads when it came time to spray paint the elementary school. He still couldn't believe Curt was serious about it.

Brad had told him second, and he timed it so that it was right before Mr. Leinenger started talking to the class and that way Curt wouldn't start bugging him. Of course, Curt began babbling right away regardless, something about telling his parents to forget about the "dumb, stupid, girlie dance recital". Apparently, Mr. Leinenger wasn't in a great mood himself because he instantly moved Curt to a seat right up front next to him. Brad had to look down for several moments to keep his grin out of sight.

So, having said his excuse twice already, Brad felt a little more comfortable by the time he told Arnie that he couldn't make it to his house. Brad was expecting Arnie to quickly and loudly argue like Curt had tried. He was surprised then, and a little nervous, when Arnie didn't say anything. Instead, he just stared at Brad, and kind of nodded his head up and down just a little.

"So, um, anyway, hope you guys have fun tonight," Brad said, being sure to frown, as he turned away from Arnie and began walking down the hall.

As he walked, he pretended to check behind him to see if someone was coming before he crossed into his class. He got a bit of a cold shiver down his neck as he saw that Arnie was still standing there, arms crossed, still staring at him.

Brad was reliving that moment as his dad pulled the family car up to the dance studio. Frannie flew out of the car in typical wildness, snapping Brad out of his thoughts. He opened his door and started to get out as well.

"Hang on, Brad. We need to go park and get out of the way of these other cars," his dad said, motioning with his head behind him.

With the last-minute panic at home of Frannie getting ready, nothing had been said about Brad going to the recital. That didn't bother him at all. So as soon has the car was shifted into park, he again started to get out.

"Brad, honey, just a second," his mom said from the front seat. The dome light from inside the car cast a shadow on her face.

"I just want you to know that I think it is very sweet of you to see your sister dance – especially when your friends are having a sleepover."

Brad was very glad the dome light went out just as she finished, otherwise she would have seen his look of surprise. How did she know he was invited to the darn sleepover? Then he remembered the phone ringing as he had dashed out of the house that morning.

"Um, yeah, Mom. Um, you're welcome. I mean, uh, yeah, I mean thanks.... yeah, thanks," Brad muttered as he fully got out of the car and shut the door – a little louder than he meant to do.

Brad tried to concentrate on the recital – he did notice there were some very cute girls up on the stage – but he kept thinking about Arnie staring at him. What the heck had he told his mom on the phone this morning? And more importantly what the heck had she told him??

On the way home Brad was very glad all the attention was aimed at Frannie. He even managed to figure out a compliment to say to her.

"Thanks," she automatically said. Then turning next to him in the backseat, more slowly added, "And I mean that."

OK, Frannie, Brad thought. I guess that's why you said it, goofball.

At home Brad started into the kitchen from the garage, then suddenly Frannie slipped past him like an eel in a coral reef and zipped to the stairs. Taking them two at a time, she was up and into her room in seconds. Brad headed toward the refrigerator. On the way he noticed the blinking red on the telephone answering machine. It looked like someone had draped a string of flashing Christmas lights on it, there were so many. Forgetting his stomach for the time being, he quickly walked into the den and slid the pocket door shut behind him.

He sat down in the swivel chair at the desk, glad that his parents were hollering questions up the stairs asking Frannie about her plans for the rest of the night. He leaned his head against the back of the chair, exhaled loudly, then leaned forward, grabbed the phone handset and pushed the play button on the answering machine his dad had added in the den. With relief, he was glad to hear that the first message was from his grandmother, wishing Frannie good luck at the recital. He started to push delete before realizing that would be dumb; the message was for his sister.

The next message was kind of garbled, sort of like the person didn't know the recording had started. Eventually there were different voices in the background and finally Brad could discern Curt's voice.

"Brat, listen. Last chance. I'm heading to Arnie's and I'm going to come by your house and get you. Be ready. Last chance." Then there was a pause and Brad figured that Curt had put the phone receiver down away from his mouth because he could faintly hear Curt say, "What? Whad'ja say?" Then louder, with the phone clearly all but in his mouth, Curt added, "And Derek said if you don't go to Arnie's you are a total loser, geek, dweeb pansy!" And with that Curt hung up. Just as quickly, Brad deleted the message.

Not sure he wanted to hear another lovely message like that one, Brad thought about walking away. But he also knew he did not want anyone else in his family hearing the garbage that was likely on there, so he again pushed play. This time it was Rudy. Brad shook his head as he could just picture Rudy trying to come across as tough, but not sure what to say as he mimicked the barbs Curt and Arnie were saying in the background. Brad hardly paid attention to the name-calling and the comments about "true friendship" and "real buddies". As he listened to Rudy's final comment, Brad actually felt bad for him for a moment.

"Seriously, Brad. Get over here." Then desperately, "Please."

As he pushed delete again, Brad mumbled, "There's your friendship."

The pinball arcade of lights had at least slowed down, but there were still two messages flashing. Brad again exhaled as he pushed play.

"So, listen, Brat," Arnie's voice boomed, "you can quit playing your little baby game, you stinking, rotten liar!" Brad was so taken aback that he pushed pause. He replayed the message just far enough to hear "…you stinking, rotten liar!" Brad stared open-mouthed at the phone in his hand. "What are you talking about??" Brad said aloud, as if Arnie was inside the handset and could answer him. After a moment, Brad let the message continue.

"Your sister told me about her demented dance recital AND, you little liar, she also told me you didn't *have* to go and nobody in your family *expected* you to go and she didn't even *want*

72

you to go, you little two-faced creep, AND you have the guts to look me in the eye...." Finally, Arnie took a breath before continuing, "...and pretend – pretend, you little weasel – that you're all sad that you can't come over to my place?! What a joke! Well, I'm glad you're not here you wimpy, pathetic.... coward! That's what you are – a coward! Heck with you!" The message finished with Arnie slamming the phone down.

Brad sat motionless, staring at the answering machine. An icy feeling appeared in his chest. His breaths started coming quicker and shorter. Arnie's words echoed in his mind, the hurtful phrases seemingly bumping into each other as they sought to wound Brad over and over.

Two-faced creep little weasel wimpy coward little liar.

Liar.

Brad wasn't sure how much time had passed when he sat up and slightly shook his head. Arnie's words seemed to have worked their way out of his mind, then somehow, they now seemed to be coming from behind the door of the den.

What?

"Oh NO!" Brad audibly gasped as he realized the answering machine in the kitchen was being played on speaker phone.

Without thinking, Brad shot up and threw the pocket door open. He could see the back half of his dad standing at the counter, the front half concealed by the kitchen counters.

Brad stood frozen as he heard, again, "That's what you are – a coward! Heck with you!"

Knowing that there was one more message, and fearing how much worse this one must be, Brad hurried into the kitchen.

"Dad, wait..." he started, but his father simply raised his left arm and held out his hand out in an unmistakable sign for Brad to stop.

Not sure what to expect, but knowing that it had to be awful, Brad braced himself for the next message.

He was surprised and then confused when, instead of one –
or all three- of the guys hurling more angry words at him, he heard
a woman's voice. Even after she identified herself, Brad had
trouble understanding that Mrs. Chestler was calling them. Still
racked with guilt about her broken sidewalk lamp, Brad oddly felt
like she was right in the kitchen talking directly to them. Head
down, he processed some of her words, ".... lots and lots of leaves
in the yard again, and I'll pay for the help, of course." There was a
pause in the message, then she chuckled a bit as she continued,
"I'm not sure what fair pay is these days, but I trust Brad."

After what seemed like too long of a time, Brad's dad
finally spoke.
"A bit ironic, isn't it?" he said quietly.
Brad wasn't sure what to do. He thought he was being
asked a question, but he really didn't understand what his dad was
asking.
"Umm…don't know," he said, instantly regretting how
dumb he sounded, even to himself.
"I think that pretending-not-to-know game you're playing
has been used enough lately, son," his dad said, looking directly at
him.
"When you go up to your room I think you'll have some
time to figure it out." Then he turned toward the kitchen and
disappeared from Brad's sight.

CHAPTER 18
FRIDAY, NOVEMBER 7
NIGHT

Brad launched himself on to his bed, back first. Grimacing, he looked up at the ceiling, gritted his teeth, and shook his head back and forth as a hissing sound escaped between his lips. He didn't know exactly what to call what he was feeling, but he knew he didn't like it.

He did know the iciness in his chest was still there, but not as strong as it had been. At the same time, weirdly he thought, there was a growing hot sensation in his stomach. Images and sounds flashed through his mind:

Arnie's loud voice bellowing ugly words over and over.

Cans of spray paint seeming to look at him, the colored lids of the cans like strange, bulging eyes.

Pleasant words of thanks from his mom and from Frannie.

Rudy anxiously repeating "please, please, please".

The look on his dad's face and in his eyes before he turned away.

Brad didn't like this feeling – these feelings – whatever you'd call it, he thought. This was new to him. He experienced a brief flashback to a time when he was little and on the merry-go-round. He knew he was supposed to enjoy it, but the up-and-down of the horse, the loud sounds of the music, all the bright colors and the shiny reflections from the mirrors were just too much for him.

He kind of felt that way now.

Brad got up from his bed and walked to the window. He hadn't shut the curtain before, and his reflection stared back at him. He didn't like what he saw. He hurriedly threw the window open and poked his head outside. Though it was cold, he liked it, needed it.

Brad didn't know how long he stood there, not really looking at anything, just trying not to think or feel. He just stood, looking out. Finally, a shiver caused by the chilly air startled him into awareness, and he closed the window as well as the curtain.

A sudden desire to have Tripp in the room with him overcame Brad. He started toward the door, then stopped when he pictured his dad holding up his left hand for him to stop. He didn't remember the exact words, but he was pretty sure he was supposed to stay in his room. He plopped down on his desk chair and without any thought reached for the magazine that lay there. He thumbed through the *Sports Illustrated for Kids* and about halfway through realized that, if asked, he couldn't tell someone about a single word or photo that he'd seen. He plunked the magazine back onto the desk.

Brad's stomach growled. He realized that he never made it to the refrigerator when they got home. He felt a flush of anger rise up his neck as he thought of the phone messages again. He wondered if he was mad because the lights on the answering machine sidetracked him from getting a snack – or because of what was said. Brad knew, but pretended to blame his hunger and anger on the distraction.

He grabbed the magazine again, then promptly put it down. He looked at the pile of books on his desk. He could get started on the book for his next book report. The thought of doing homework on a Friday night kind of grossed him out, though. Regardless, he reached for *Hatchet* and lay down on the bed. He opened the cover and turned pages until he got to the first chapter. He read the first sentence, then found himself looking over the top of the book to the ceiling. He started looking at the shapes and designs up there, as he had done a hundred times. Eventually, he became aware of his eyes closing then opening, and his head bobbing down and then snapping alert. Then, despite trying to stay awake because he felt he was supposed to, Brad fell asleep.

CHAPTER 19
SATURDAY, NOVEMBER 8
MORNING

In Brad's dream, he was riding some type of carousel horse, trying to get it to speed up, encouraging it to get away from horses behind him – horses that strangely had heads like people. People like Arnie, Curt and – oddly – Derek. As if that wasn't bizarre enough, Brad could hear Tripp barking somewhere in the commotion. His barking was loud and insistent, as if he too was urging the horses to move quicker. Tripp's barking became louder and more dominant, overtaking the visual of the merry-go-round scene and drowning out all other sounds in the picture. Gradually, Brad started to emerge from this vision, and he felt himself between a dream state and reality. But Tripp's barking continued, louder and louder.

Pushing Brad the rest of the way out of his sleep, his dad's voice called from the backyard, "Tripp- hush it! You're never going to catch that squirrel anyway."

Brad sat up and leaned on his elbows. He shook his head a bit, trying to clear the fogginess that persisted. Confused, he looked down and saw that he was wearing the same clothes that he had worn to Frannie's dance recital. He wasn't even under the covers, and he wondered for a moment if it was still night. But the bright daylight dismissed that possibility, and Brad knew then it was morning.

Almost fully awake now, Brad kicked his feet to the floor and, after a momentary bit of instability, stood up. His bladder and his gurgling stomach combined to push him out the door. After taking care of business, he left the bathroom and headed down the stairs to the kitchen.

"Oh, good morning, Brad!" his mom sang, a bit too loudly Brad thought. He nodded his head and muttered, "Morning…"

He went to the pantry and grabbed a box of Life cereal, then a bowl from a cabinet, a spoon from a drawer, milk from the refrigerator, a banana from the counter and was heading to the table when he heard the door from the garage open. Managing to cradle all the items against his chest, he pivoted to see his dad step into the kitchen.

His dad didn't notice him right away as he stomped remnant pieces of leaves off his shoes, but when he did he chuckled as he said, "Nice pajamas, son."

Brad glanced down over the milk carton at his left shirt sleeve while he realized that his dad had noticed he had slept in his clothes.

Chuckling again, his dad said, "Go ahead and sit down. I'd hate to see all that drop to the floor."

Brad moved to the table and squatted down as he eased everything onto the surface. He wasn't sure what to expect next. Would his dad say something right away about the phone messages – and everything else? Should he start trying to explain stuff? He did not want to do that because he had no idea where to start and how much to say. He stood there silently as these thoughts bounced around his head. He glanced over to his dad, who stood just inside the door, arms crossed.

"You better get started on breakfast because right after you're done we're heading to Mrs. Chestler's."

Oh.

Brad remembered her phone message. She had said something about raking leaves again and him setting the price. He quickly thought of the broken light, and he shot a sideways glance at his dad. Mr. Bateman stood as before, arms still crossed, but his chuckling grin was replaced by a different expression; lips tight together and brow wrinkled slightly, eyes intently studying his son. Brad got the distinct feeling that his dad was trying to figure out exactly what Brad knew but hadn't said yet. Dreading a question about all that, Brad hurriedly sat down and launched into his breakfast.

As they pulled up to Mrs. Chestler's house, Brad strained to see the condition of the light fixture. He couldn't spot anything broken this time and was relieved to think that maybe it was already fixed. He opened the car door and went to the tailgate. Brad grabbed the rake, leaf bags and gloves. His dad shut the tailgate and Brad thought for a moment that he would hop back behind the steering wheel and drive away. Instead, his dad walked up the sidewalk just as Mrs. Chestler was stepping out the front door onto the porch.

"Good morning!" he said enthusiastically.

"Oh, good morning to both of you," she replied. "Bless your hearts for coming over here."

Brad's father turned toward Brad and gave a slight nod of his head toward Mrs. Chestler, then raised his eyebrows and cocked his head that way again when Brad hadn't said anything.

"Oh, yeah, right. Um, you're welcome......" Brad said, his inflection rising a bit at the end almost as if it was a question.

Brad's dad looked at him another moment, a slightly bemused look on his face.

Turning back to Mrs. Chestler, he said, "Your trees must produce more leaves than any other trees in the world!"

She laughed and said, "I do believe you're right. It doesn't seem to end."

Surprising Brad, his father then said, "Well, the new light sure looks good," as he walked up to it.

Brad quickly walked to the open garage door, pulled out the trash can, and began shaking open one of the trash bags to put inside.

"Yes, thanks," she replied. "Though they didn't have a globe exactly the same as the other ones."

"I didn't even notice," he commented, closely inspecting the light up close. "Brad, what do you think? Can you notice a difference?"

Caught off guard, Brad's eyes darted from the new light fixture to the next closest one. "Ah, not really. It looks good, about the same, better…. but not *that* different. I guess." And then he turned to go get the rake. He purposely walked to the far corner of the front yard, away from the adults and his dad's car.

"Mrs. Chestler said you can use her phone when you're done," his dad called as he slid into the driver's seat of his car.

Though the amount of leaves to rake up was daunting and he would have liked having his dad split the work, Brad was relieved that his dad left. He can tell I know about the broken light, Brad thought, as he pulled the first of what would be many piles of leaves toward himself. I mean how obvious is it when he goes up to the new light and asks if I can tell the difference between that one and the old ones? And what was that he said last night about Mrs. Chestler saying she could trust me? And oh yeah, Dad said something about me playing some game about pretending not to know.

These questions and thoughts were joined by others as Brad continued working. He got into a rhythm of raking the leaves into piles, shoving them in the bags that lined the trash can, stepping inside the trash can to smash down the leaves, pulling the filled bags out, hauling those to the side of the garage, putting a new bag in the trash can, and starting the process over again. As his body repeated the motions almost automatically, his mind went in a dozen different directions.

He already realized that somehow his dad had figured out about the light. But then with a bit of panic, Brad suddenly wondered if his dad thought *he* broke it! Brad made one decision right then: he would tell his dad that Curt broke the light, not him.

Brad stopped working for a moment, holding the top of the rake handle with both hands. Looking in the direction of the new light, but not really seeing it, he played out different possibilities and situations in his mind. What will his dad say when he tells on Curt? What if Curt finds out? What does his dad know about the spray painting? Brad whispered aloud, "I didn't have anything to do with painting either school!" His thoughts continued. Why should I say anything? Besides how incredibly mad would Arnie and Curt be if they found out I said something? And oh-my-gosh, what would Derek and Sweet say – or DO – to me if *they* found out??

Almost as if they were said aloud directly into his ears, Brad became aware of the words SUPPRESS THE TRUTH.

"What the heck!" he said loudly, frustrated that none of this was simple and the whole thing kept getting more complicated.

Brad jumped slightly when he heard, "What's that you say, Brad?"

Surprised, he turned to see Mrs. Chestler holding a tray with some type of bread and a glass.

"You've been working so hard, I thought you might like some pumpkin bread and apple juice," she said. "I just took the bread out of the oven."

Just then the amazing smell hit Brad, and he dropped the rake and reached out for a piece.

"Yes!" he said, "That smells great! Thanks very much."

Without any words necessary, they both walked to the front porch and sat down. Brad dived into a second piece of bread, only realizing after it was halfway eaten that he probably should have waited for Mrs. Chestler to offer it to him. She slowly was still eating her first piece when Brad finished his last bite. Brad was thinking about having a third piece and glanced up at Mrs. Chestler. As he did, he noticed the new, repaired light fixture visible just past her profile. He sat looking at it and might have kept looking longer if Mrs. Chestler hadn't turned toward him, a pleasant grin on her face. Not wanting her to think he was staring at her, he quickly reached down to the little table between them and grabbed the glass off the tray. Looking straight ahead, he downed two-thirds of the apple juice in one gulp.

Surprising himself, he suddenly said, "I know who broke your light," motioning with his head toward the fixture.

"Oh?" she said.

"Um, yeah." He glanced up briefly and she was calmly looking his way. Realizing he couldn't just stop there, he continued, "It was Curt Compton," the words coming unexpectedly easy.

"Oh?" she said again.

"Yeah," and quickly added, "but he didn't mean to."

"Oh?" she said a third time.

Brad looked over at her a moment. When he did, Mrs. Chestler asked, "Well now, how do you know that?"

Immediately understanding that he had set himself up for this, Brad exhaled audibly and looked out over the yard, which was now thankfully mostly cleared of leaves.

He took a deep breath and blew it out loudly between his pursed lips.

"He meant to just throw your pumpkin down and smash it, but when he threw it the light was in the way – and he hit it. And he broke it."

"Oh?" she asked yet again.

Pausing, Brad said quietly, looking down, "Yeah. I was with him."

"I know," Mrs. Chestler said softly.

Still looking down, Brad blinked twice, then jerked his head up toward her.

She sat still, hands folded in her lap, with one side of her mouth slightly raised in an almost-grin.

"I was looking out this window," she said, motioning behind her with a slight movement of her head.

"You boys run fast!" she said with a laugh.

Brad couldn't help but chuckle himself.

Processing what this meant, Brad said, "So….my parents? They know, too?"

She simply nodded her head.

"How long?"

This time Mrs. Chestler looked forward. She too took a somewhat deep breath, and turning to Brad, said, "I think that's a question they should answer."

CHAPTER 20
SUNDAY, NOVEMBER 9
MORNING

"I'm sure, absolutely sure, *everyone* has started on the homework assignment I gave in youth group last week, right?" Pastor Dan said, his eyebrows dancing up and down mischievously and a smirk on his face.

With a bit of panic in his voice, Nathan Fenton quickly said, "But you clearly stated that this assignment would not be due until our next *youth group* meeting, which isn't until Wednesday, December 3rd." Taking a breath, his voice noticeably higher, Nathan added, "This is obviously *Sunday School* and NOT youth group."

Trying to suppress a laugh, Pastor Dan held both his hands out in a "calm down" gesture, and said, "As is often the case, you are exactly right, Nathan." Then briefly looking around the circle, seemingly to assess the other kids' reactions, Pastor Dan continued, "I certainly didn't want to worry anyone when I asked that." Looking around once again, he added lightly, "I'm just curious."

Realizing that the comments were aimed at him, and noticing that everyone else was smiling – or at least not looking worried – Nathan forced a nervous laugh and stammered, "That's good, yes, yes, that's good. Good."

With everyone looking at Nathan, who fidgeted awkwardly and tried to force a smile, Pastor Dan right away said, "Well, obviously some of you – or maybe all of you – have not yet found the time to talk with your parents about the whole topic of truth."

Seeing several nodding heads, he added, "That's OK, of course." He paused, then looked over the heads of the kids across from him for a few moments. Nodding his head as if to confirm whatever he was thinking, he continued, "I am convinced that it will be a valuable conversation – whenever you're able to have it." He paused again, seeming to ask himself a question. Then he asked, "Anyone talk to their parents yet?"

With no hesitation, Brad nodded his head.

Pastor Dan noticed and raised his eyebrows a bit as he asked Brad,

"How did it go?"

"Really long," Brad replied, to which everyone laughed.

After the giggling subsided, Pastor Dan said, "No pressure, Brad – but is there anything you want to share? Any surprises?"

Brad had been surprised to learn that his dad had lied to his parents when he got home late from a date in high school. Brad wasn't sure if he was more surprised by the lie or the fact that his dad had actually dated someone other than his mom. Weird, he thought. And he had been really surprised to learn that his mom had lied once to her mother about taking two cookies out of the cookie jar when she was little. He still couldn't picture his mom doing anything wrong.

But he didn't feel right about telling his parents' stories. Actually, as he thought about it, he again had the feeling he'd experienced yesterday, kind of like growing closer to his parents because of what they'd shared with him.

He also did not want to get into the whole jack-o-lantern-breaking-the-light thing, and he especially did not want to say anything about the stupid graffiti again.

Carefully, Brad did manage to say, "I just know I felt different after we talked."

"Different as in better or worse?"

"Definitely better."

"Better in what way?"

"Lighter, kind of."

"Interesting! Lighter…. like, what exactly do you mean, Brad?"

Brad looked up at the ceiling, searching for the right way to describe what he meant.

"Like I wasn't carrying around a bunch of … I don't know, like sharp rocks in my stomach anymore."

Nobody said anything, and Brad looked down, wondering if he'd messed up by saying what he had.

Finally, someone across the circle said, "I know exactly what you mean."

Brad looked up where the voice came from and saw a smile and what he felt was a look of admiration on Ashley Sherman's face.

Brad thought about what else he did not tell this group: the assignments from his parents. He sort of accomplished part of what they made him commit to doing by telling the kids here that he felt better – lighter – after talking about telling the truth with his parents. His mom and dad would probably agree that was pretty much the same as their first requirement: to tell other kids that being honest isn't just right, it helps the person who is being honest. Of course, telling kids in a Sunday School class is different than telling kids at regular school, Brad acknowledged, but still….

Brad felt a sense of pride as he replayed the second part of what his parents insisted he do. Without his parents telling him to, Brad had refused any money from Mrs. Chestler. She was stubborn, but he finally convinced her she had paid him when he took that third piece of pumpkin bread. He even accepted her offer to go inside and get him another glass of apple juice. His parents had seemed proud of him, and their smiles even gave Brad the confidence to joke, "Sorry that I can't give you the satisfaction of seeing me take back the money."

Brad felt a little shiver run down his back, though, as he thought about the third assignment, the really hard thing his parents were making him do.

He'd have to take care of that later.

CHAPTER 21
MONDAY, NOVEMBER 10
MORNING

Ms. Cruz loudly said, "Listen up! Class, I want everyone looking at me – STARING at me – right now!" She enthusiastically pointed both her index fingers directly at her own eyes and rotated her head around the room.

"Let me see those beautiful peepers. Everyone!"

Of course, that's all it took for most of the class of 6th grade kids to lean forward, bug-eyed as goldfish as they followed the teacher's orders.

"Goodness," she exclaimed, "I don't want anyone straining their brains – or their eyes – but I DO want you to continue looking at me as I explain what we're going to be doing."

After scanning the room to make sure all the students were paying attention to her, she continued, "We're going to play a little game here. I'm going to say a certain word in a minute, and if you can continue to look at me, and listen to me, then you're going to be able to make some of your own choices."

Ms. Cruz instantly went on, "Buuuuut...anyone – ANY ONE! - who looks away from me when I say this particular word – even for a second – ONE second, people! – will lose their right to choose."

Putting her fingers down finally, she continued, "Moral of the story? Keep watching me, friends."

"Yo, what's the magic word?" Arnie asked loudly, and Curt chuckled, but he was the only one.

"I am getting there, Arnold," Ms. Cruz replied, and several people snickered at her use of his full name.

"Remembering that you need to look at me – and not at anyone else – I'm going to tell you the…. *special* word."

Pausing to again check that each kid was tuned in, she said quietly, "The word that I'm going to say will interest you social young people, so one more time, remember to look at me when I tell you the word is…. 'Group'. Good job maintaining eye contact, kids! Keep looking at me as I go on."

Ms. Cruz went on to explain that they were going to be assigned a group project for the next two weeks. Since everyone somehow managed to look at her and not get a head start on selecting their group members, she said they each could choose two or three classmates with whom to work when she gave them the OK.

Brad felt a lump in his stomach.

He felt like the eyes of Arnie, Curt, and Rudy were drilling holes into the back of his head. He truly did not want to be in a group with them.

Brad sat frozen for a bit, not sure what he should do. Instinctively, he dropped his pencil and, as he bent in his chair to retrieve it, he craned his neck backward to sneak a look in Arnie's direction. Brad was both relieved and a bit stunned when he realized that Arnie was not looking his direction; in fact, his back was turned toward Brad. To his right stood Curt and to his left was Rudy. Neither one of them looked his way either. Connecting the circle of four together was the same tall boy Arnie was with, who apparently must be Sweet's cousin, Brad thought.

Sitting up in his seat again, Brad looked ahead, realizing what this meant. He wasn't going to be in a group with those guys. He was glad about that. Mostly.

So, who would be in his group? This was a new feeling to him.

He understood suddenly that he was going to have to do something about getting into a group for this project. Nervously, he tilted his head to the side to see if all the kids were already matched up. It seemed like it. Slowly turning his head to look the other way, he saw four arms in the corner, almost frantic as they waved back and forth. It took him a second to put together that two of the arms belonged to Nathan and two to Ashley. When they both saw that Brad noticed them, each of them began motioning him over to that corner of the room. He hesitated a second, then grabbed his backpack from underneath his chair and headed over.

Brad started to say 'Hey' when he got closer, but Nathan enthusiastically called, "Hi, Brad! Want to be in our group? It's Ashley and me. If you say 'yes' it will be the three of us! Want to?"

Brad was embarrassed how loud Nathan was, and he could tell a few people noticed and were watching. He quickly grabbed an empty chair and slid into it after pulling it nearer to the two of them.

Brad grasped the idea that he really didn't have any options at this point. He couldn't fake the same level of excitement that Nathan obviously felt, but Brad didn't want to seem like a snob. So he said, "Yeah, that'll be good," smiling slightly.

After seeing the beaming smile on Nathan's face, he added, "Um, thanks."

"Thank you!" Nathan eagerly replied.

Brad didn't feel comfortable. He always felt like Nathan treated him like some hero or something. Brad wished he didn't.

Brad glanced over where Arnie and the others sat. They were laughing at something and seemed very happy about the whole situation.

Ashley noticed Brad, and she gently said, "I'm glad you're in this group, Brad."

Turning toward her, Brad wasn't sure what to say. She smiled at him, then she looked away when Brad didn't respond.

After an awkward silence, Brad quietly said, "Yeah. This is good. I mean we'll do good – er, I mean we'll do well."

Without realizing it, Brad again glanced back toward the four boys.

Ashley said, "I think it's time."

Brad tentatively asked, "Time to…. start on our project?"

"No. It's time to break up 'CRAB'."

Feeling very confused, Brad looked at Ashley hoping somehow her face would let him know what the heck she was talking about.

It didn't help.

"So…I don't get it," he finally said.

"CRAB, Brad," she said matter-of-factly.

When Brad still didn't respond, she added, "The name that describes your group?"

"Huh?" he said, sounding dumber than he wanted to.

"Seriously?" Ashley asked incredulously.

Seeing Brad just shaking his head slightly, Ashley went on.

"CRAB. C for Curt, R for Rudy, A for Arnie, and, of course, B for you – Brad," she finished, smiling widely.

Brad stared at her open-mouthed for several moments.

Seeing the look on his face, Ashley's smile began to fade.

Brad continued looking at her, and when he finally noticed she wasn't smiling, he asked, "So how long have you been saying that?"

Ashley wiggled nervously in her seat a bit, then turned toward Nathan.

"Remember back in first grade when we studied the ocean?" Nathan asked.

Brad nodded.

Then he began to comprehend what Nathan was saying.

"You called us CRAB since first grade?!" he asked dubiously.

Ashley and Nathan together just nodded their heads but said nothing.

Just then, a loud sound grabbed everyone's attention. All three of them turned to see Arnie on the floor, his chair on top of him. The other three boys were laughing hysterically and pointing at Arnie. Brad had seen Arnie tipping back in his chair and falling so many times in the past that he knew exactly what had happened.

91

Ms. Cruz calmly walked over there, and Brad turned back around to again face his new group members.

"Wow," Ashley said.

"What?" Nathan and Brad asked simultaneously.

"I just thought of something." She paused, then grinned as she said, "The name of that new boy in their group is Paul. Paul with a 'P'. I guess the name of that group no longer is CRA*B*," she giggled, emphasizing the 'B' sound.

Brad and Nathan both caught on at the same time, and all three of them laughed together.

CHAPTER 22
MONDAY, NOVEMBER 10
AFTERNOON

Brad was really glad the weather was decent. It wasn't exactly warm, but a few kids chose to eat lunch outside. He wouldn't be noticed like he would be if he was the only kid not staying in the cafeteria. Still, he was careful to use the door furthest away from where the guys sat as he walked quickly over to the tree where he had sat last week. Again, he put his back against the side of the tree that faced away from the school windows. This time he carefully set his backpack down instead of hurling it.

He reached into the pack to pull out his lunch. Instead of touching the lunch bag first, something else hit his hand. Brad pulled it out and read the outside of the envelope that was labeled 'Mr. Andrews' in Brad's handwriting. He gulped a bit as he recalled having to write the letter Saturday night. His dad first told Brad he would have to talk to Mr. Andrews in person. The panic that he had felt when he heard that came rushing back to Brad. He relived using his most convincing words to talk his parents into letting him write a letter instead. It would have been awful talking to Mr. Andrews. He'd ask a ton of questions! I guess all that persuasive writing Mrs. Seversen has us do in English is paying off, Brad thought.

He glanced down at the envelope again. "Oh, man…" he whispered. He once again flashed through different things that could happen if anyone found out what he had written. Realizing that anyone seeing the assistant principal's name on an envelope would probably wonder what was inside, Brad urgently shoved it back into the backpack. He double checked that no one was around, then reached in for his lunch.

His original plan was to stop by the office to deliver it before going to the cafeteria. There was no way that was going to work he discovered, as a continuous movement of kids snaked in and out of the office doorway. Brad never knew so many kids took meds at school – or whatever else they were doing. As he took a bite of his sandwich, he thought about another plan. He couldn't ask to leave English class, which was after lunch. All three of the guys were also in that class, and he realized the new kid – Paul – was, too. At least one of them would notice and pester him about where he had gone. He finished the first half of his sandwich. His next class was art. None of the other guys were in there. But he suddenly saw Nathan's face in his mind. Even though he sat on the other side of the room, he would absolutely notice if Brad left. And he'd ask a bunch of annoying questions later. P.E. was his last class. It was harder to remember who was in that class because they didn't have assigned seats, or any seat at all actually. He pictured Friday's dodge ball game, starting with who was on the other team and then circling back in his mind to his teammates. None of them – including Nathan – were in that class. Just as he was thinking he could get this painful chore over with, he realized that no one ever brought their backpack to P.E. He'd totally stand out if he dragged his in to the gym. He couldn't risk putting the letter in his pocket because it could fall out – especially with all the moving around they did in P.E. class.

Brad took a big bite of his apple. As he chewed, he considered another possibility. He could stick around after school and deliver the letter to one of secretaries in the office. But just as soon as he thought of this, he knew there would be a bunch of people hanging around. Even if it wasn't one of the boys he was most concerned about, middle school kids were nosy. Somebody would tell somebody else about him being there. Mr. Andrews was always out by the buses, trying to keep the craziness down as much as possible. There was no way he could hand the envelope straight to Mr. Andrews outside, though. Brad shuddered as he pictured

Mr. Andrews booming with his ridiculously loud voice, "Well, what do you have here for me, Mr. Bateman? Why, it looks like a letter! Let's read it, shall we?! 'Dear Mr. Andrews....'"

Uh, NO, Brad thought.

So, he would just have to deliver it tomorrow. He'd wait until about halfway through math class when they usually had time to start working on the assignment. Most kids who even noticed would assume he was just using the bathroom, and there weren't any kids in this class he had to worry about. He just hoped his parents would understand without him having to go through every minute of the day explaining why it didn't get done. He might have to be persuasive, he thought, smiling to himself.

CHAPTER 23
TUESDAY, NOVEMBER 11
MORNING

Brad's parents were at a meeting Monday night, so the letter to Mr. Andrews wasn't mentioned in the few minutes they were together. Brad kind of felt like he was getting away with something. Before sitting down to breakfast, he had a quick impulse to grab a granola bar and hurriedly dash out the door. Kind of a Frannie trick. But then he remembered his dad saying, "I think that pretending-not-to-know game you're playing has been used enough lately, son." This wasn't exactly the same, but avoiding the discussion wasn't really honest either. So Brad sat down.

Brad's dad came rushing down the stairs just then and said, "I've just got time to grab a cup of coffee and whatever I can take with me." Mrs. Bateman handed him a travel mug and a couple of granola bars. I wonder if that is ironic that he's the one leaving in a hurry, Brad thought to himself.

The door to the garage was thrown open, then just as rapidly as he had gone out, Mr. Bateman popped back in partway.

"You got that letter delivered OK, Brad?" he hastily asked, smiling.

Brad knew his dad was running late, and he didn't want to make something up, so he hurriedly replied, "I'm going to do it in my first class today!"

His dad frowned, looked at his wife, then back at Brad before saying, "I sure hope there's a good explanation. And you start telling your mom right now. I'll be talking to her later this morning." With that, the door closed.

Before his mom could say anything, Brad started, "There is a good explanation, Mom."

"Oh?" she asked, and Brad wondered just how much Mrs. Chestler and his parents talk together since his mom suddenly sounded a lot like her.

"Basically, there's almost always somebody around who would be nosy. You know, the CRAB guys. I mean the CRA..." and Brad blushed a bit as he noticed his mom's confused expression.

"Well, anyway, today in math none of .... those guys are in that class, so when it's work time I'll just ask Mr. Garcia if I can run something to the office."

"We had a deal, Brad," his mom said.

"Yes, we do, AND," Brad said emphasizing the word 'and' as he remembered Mrs. Seversen saying it's more persuasive to say 'Yes, *and*' instead of 'Yes, *but*', "I will get my part of the deal done right away!"

His mom smiled a bit and said, "Are you becoming a schmoozer, Bradley Bateman?"

Not sure what she meant exactly, Brad answered, "Maybe I am."

Math class started like it always did with Mr. Garcia randomly picking kids to share their homework answers and sometimes asking them to explain how they solved it. Brad did not feel cheated when his problem was basic enough that it really didn't need an explanation. Mr. Garcia reviewed the process for renaming compound fractions again, went through a few sample problems, and then let the kids begin working on the assignment. Subtly, he motioned for a few students to join him for more instruction. As his teacher arranged chairs for the small group, Brad used that time to briefly ask him if he could quickly take a letter from home to the office. Brad had first thought about asking to use the bathroom, but he didn't see the point of not being totally honest. And it *was* a letter from home – just one that he wrote, rather than his parents.

As Brad left the room, he turned his head briefly in both directions to be sure no one was there. While he walked toward the office he found himself hoping that Mr. Andrews was busy and that he could ask a secretary to give the letter to him later. As he approached the office he leaned his head over to see if Mr. Andrews' office door was open or closed. Brad was relieved when he saw it was shut. He walked into the main office, and just as he did so Mr. Andrews came charging out of his office and stopped at the counter. He began quietly but urgently speaking to the secretary. In the space behind Mr. Andrews, Brad was shocked to see Curt sitting there in the A.P.'s office. He looked especially small in the big upholstered chair as he sat staring at the floor in front of him. As Brad looked closer he could see that Curt's left eye and cheek were badly bruised and red. Sudden pity came over Brad, and he wanted to say something. Curt hadn't looked up, and Brad suddenly became aware of the envelope in his hand. He frantically shoved it into his back pocket, hoping Curt didn't see it.

Mr. Andrews turned abruptly and almost ran into Brad, who hastily stepped back out of the way.

"Never mind calling him down," Mr. Andrews exclaimed. "I want to go get him myself." With that he bolted out of the office.

Curt looked up at the commotion, and his eyes met Brad's. Curt immediately put his left hand over the left side of his face, and he turned so that his right cheek was facing out. Brad stood motionless, not sure what to say or do.

He became aware of someone asking, "May I help you?" He looked up at Mrs. Johnson, who had gotten out of her chair and was leaning on the counter toward him.

Brad turned to his left and saw that Curt was still looking away from the office door. Nevertheless, Brad took two steps up to the counter and he checked that Curt could not see him. He carefully pulled the envelope out of his back pocket, keeping it against his side as he brought it up to the counter. Not wanting Curt to hear what he was saying, he simply pointed to the name on the envelope and said, "This is from home."

Perhaps understanding the circumstances, Mrs. Johnson simply said, "Thank you," as she took it from Brad.

Brad turned to leave, then stopped. He felt like he should say something to Curt. When Brad looked toward him all he saw was the closed door. Curt doesn't want to hear anything from me, Brad thought.

Brad did not get much work done on his math assignment. His paper did have a lot of doodles on it, however. Curt was not in music class. Brad was glad that Mr. Leinenger now had assigned places based on different parts for the Christmas concert, and Rudy was a few rows away from him. He wasn't sure what Rudy knew about Curt, if anything. But Brad sped to science right after music just in case Rudy wanted to talk about the whole thing. Rudy got confused easily, and Brad didn't want to be a part of any rumors.

It was colder that day than Monday. Brad wasn't sure he would have gone outside for lunch even if it was nicer. But he didn't quite know where to sit in the cafeteria. He recalled that he hadn't sat at the usual table with the guys since early last week. When he looked over there he saw Rudy sitting across from Paul, and neither one of them looked like they were having much fun. Still no Curt, and now no Arnie.

Brad pretended not to notice Nathan waving at him from the corner. He felt kind of bad about it, but he walked right on outside. It was uncomfortably cold, and only a few 8th grade boys were out there. Brad noticed that they seemed to be trying hard to act like they weren't freezing. Brad was, so he chomped down his sandwich in record time and headed back inside. Students weren't supposed to eat in the library, but that's where he decided to go. He shoved the rest of his lunch bag into the bottom of his backpack.

Brad scarched for as concealed a spot as possible once he was in the library. All the cushioned chairs were taken, but he did find a wooden one by itself behind some tall book cases. He moved the chair where he could sit and look out a nearby window if he stretched a bit.

He was lost in his thoughts, wondering what was going on with Curt. And now Arnie was not around either, apparently. Brad was a bit ashamed to admit to himself that, while he was concerned about Curt's black eye, he was also kind of worried that he might look bruised like that, too, if somehow this had anything to do with telling about the graffiti.

Looking aimlessly out the window, Brad was startled when he heard a quiet voice say, "You are not an easy person to find!"

He looked up and it took Brad a minute to figure out that the person standing there was Mrs. Johnson from the office.

She softly spoke again. "I gave the envelope to Mr. Andrews for you."

"Thanks," Brad barely whispered.

"Of course," she said. "He would like to talk with you – if you're OK with that," she added with a brief smile.

Oh brother! Brad thought. This is just what I did not want to happen.

As if reading his thoughts, Mrs. Johnson leaned in closer and said, "I'd like to suggest that I leave first, and I'll take a route behind these book shelves and come out clear over there," pointing well away from where Brad was sitting.

"Then in a few minutes you could walk that direction," she continued, pointing the opposite way. "No one would ever know we're heading to the same place." She took two steps, then turned and, smiling, whispered, "It will be kind of a spy thing."

Brad managed a brief smile back. She's pretty cool, he thought.

CHAPTER 24
TUESDAY, NOVEMBER 11
EVENING

"So, you got sent to see Old Man Andrews?!" Frannie all but shouted right before putting a huge forkful of salad in her mouth.

"First of all, Frannie, 'Old Man Andrews' is probably a few years younger than your mom and me," said her dad, playfully pointing his fork at her. "So, watch it!"

He looked at Brad a moment before saying, "And secondly, your brother is pretty brave being this honest in front of all of us. So, if you want to stay to hear the rest of this, I suggest you use your mouth only for food – but maybe just not so much of it at once," he added.

Frannie tried to respond, but then just nodded her head when she realized speaking would be impossible with nearly half a head of lettuce in her mouth.

Motioning to Frannie with his index finger over his own mouth just to be sure, Mr. Bateman then said, "Go ahead, son. What did Mr. Andrews say?"

Brad reached down to pat Tripp's head, then spoke faintly. "Well, he read my letter out loud – well, most of it. He said he learned that I was afraid that something bad would happen if Derek or Sweet found out that I told on them."

Brad swallowed and looked down a moment before continuing.

"Then he said something bad did happen." Brad stopped. He started fiddling with his napkin.

"Take your time," his mom said.

Taking a deep breath, Brad went on, "So, yeah, apparently Sweet has a younger cousin, Paul, in 6th grade. Which is a whole other story," Brad mumbled.

He continued, growing louder, "So Paul starts telling Sweet that Curt had been bragging about the graffiti. Curt tried to deny it, but Sweet gets mad then hauls off and punches Curt in the face!"

His mom gasped a bit, and Brad kept going, faster now. "So then Derek wasn't happy about his little brother getting smacked – even though he was also ticked off at Curt for running his mouth – so Derek hits Sweet, and they get into a big fight."

"Ohmygod!" exclaimed Frannie, a chunk of salad zinging out of her mouth. "That's why those two weren't in school!"

"Frannie, watch yourself," cautioned her dad. "One more word and you're gone."

She meekly nodded her head.

"Mr. Andrews told me that letting him know about the vandalism was the right thing to do," said Brad. His parents both smiled at him.

"But I kind of got the feeling that he thinks that if I had told him right away that maybe Curt wouldn't have gotten hurt."

"Why's that, honey?" asked his mom.

"Not sure. Maybe because they would have gotten Derek and Sweet earlier – and maybe arrested them or something. I don't know."

"Well, they will have legal consequences," remarked Mr. Bateman. "Did they have proof before your letter?"

"I guess. He did say that he kind of suspected it was those two guys."

"What I don't get is why Arnie wasn't at school," said Mrs. Bateman.

Starting to warm up a bit to this role of being Answer Man, Brad replied, "Well, it turns out that Curt wouldn't admit that his brother and his friend actually did the graffiti. When Mr. Andrews asked Curt why he wouldn't turn them in, especially after he had already told him he got beat up last night, Curt said that he didn't want to get hit by Arnie, too."

"What?!" all three seemed to ask at the same time.

"Yeah, I guess right before I got to the office Curt said to Mr. Andrews that Arnie had told Curt before school that if he 'ratted' on Derek and Sweet that he – Arnie – would beat him up, too!"

"Oh brother!" said Mr. Bateman. "What a mess,"

"Yeah, so I'm pretty sure Arnie is suspended for making threats," Brad added.

"So how come Curt wasn't in school? Was he suspended, too?" asked Mrs. Bateman.

"No. I guess it took a while for Mr. Andrews to get a hold of either of Curt's parents, but he said he should go home and heal. Plus, I don't think he wanted Curt to have to answer a ton of questions about his face."

"Wow," Mr. Bateman managed to say. "You've had quite a day."

"Yep. Pretty crazy."

"One more thing," said his dad. "What about the graffiti on Wabash? Aren't Arnie, Curt, and Rudy going to get in big trouble for that?"

"Get this! They never spray painted that school! Curt did admit they threatened to do it, but he said they were afraid that I would tell on them."

"Interesting. Well, son, I guess that's a good reputation to have."

Frannie raised her hand, as if she were in class.

Chuckling, her dad said, "Yes, Miss Bateman. What do you have to say?"

With a dramatic pause first, Frannie said, "So, Brad, I know I thanked you Friday for coming to my dance recital. Of course, I *thought* it was because you might actually have been interested in, you know, my *dancing*. But even though you actually went for another reason, I'm still really glad you were there."

She started to get up, then stopped and said, "And, Mom and Dad, of course I know that NONE of this info leaves this house."

CHAPTER 25
WEDNESDAY, NOVEMBER 12
MORNING

Brad was actually relieved when his dad insisted that he give Brad a ride to school that morning. Brad felt he had been pretty convincing in saying 'no' when he had started putting on his bike helmet, but when his dad opened the garage door and pointed to the snow that had started falling it was easier to give in and get in the car.

When his dad started pulling in to the drop-off zone in front of school, though, Brad pleaded with him to pull up further on Mae Boulevard, so he could get out and walk. Even then, he hoped no one noticed that he had gotten a ride. He purposely took off his knit cap, getting snow on his head to look authentic.

As he entered the front door of the school, Brad felt a bit like one of the cows he had seen being herded during a family summer trip through farmland. The sounds of boots stamping off snow could almost pass as the mooing of cattle. Brad found himself being jostled along with the crowd. It wasn't until he was just about at the main office that he realized he needed to go the other direction to get to his locker. Brad smiled sheepishly when he remembered that one of the many thoughts that kept him awake last night was a concern about being near the office. He had worried that if someone had seen him near there, they would automatically connect him to Mr. Andrews and the graffiti situation. He chuckled because there was such a mob that no individual could be noticed.

He eventually made his way to his locker, hung up the damp coat and grabbed the books he needed. The thinning crowd told him he needed to hurry to class.

Math went fine, and again Curt was not in music. He made a point to avoid looking at Rudy. Not sure what to expect in geography, Brad hesitated a moment before making a beeline to where he had sat with Ashley and Nathan. He barely had time to say hi before Ms. Cruz called for their attention. Turning toward her, Brad quickly glanced where the four boys had sat Monday. Four chairs were arranged together, but only two were occupied. Rudy sat across from Paul, whose back faced Ms. Cruz despite her asking a second time for everyone to look at her. Brad noticed that Rudy slumped in his chair with his arms crossed right after Paul did. Both sat with their heads down.

Brad was not surprised that as soon as Ms. Cruz finished explaining the directions for the day, Nathan instantly started suggesting what each of them could do for the project. Brad was fine with whatever part he had, as long as Nathan didn't say a word about anything to do with Mr. Andrews, graffiti, Arnie, Curt, or anything else, really. Brad always figured Nathan knew everything about everything, so he was surprised that Nathan seemed unaware of what had happened. Brad was glad about that.

A couple of times during class Brad stole glances toward Rudy and Paul. They had moved a bit closer together, but now both of their backs angled toward Brad. When Brad looked up he saw that Ashley was looking intently at him. He decided he didn't need to peek at Rudy and Paul anymore.

CHAPTER 26
WEDNEDAY, NOVEMBER 12
AFTERNOON

It had stopped snowing by lunch time. Still, no one was allowed to go outside - even after they ate. Brad ended up sitting with Nathan, Jermaine Robinson, and a couple of other boys he didn't know very well. He only knew Jermaine from church, but because he hadn't gone to Wabash for elementary school and Brad didn't have any classes with him, Brad never spent time with Jermaine. The four other boys talked the whole time about a new video game they apparently each had gotten. This didn't bother Brad at all. As long as nothing was said about the whole other mess, he was fine.

When the lunch period was over Brad stood up to leave the cafeteria. As he did, he happened to see Paul pointing at him and then laughing as he said something to Rudy. Brad recognized Rudy's forced response. He'd seen it a hundred times before when someone – usually Arnie – said something that Rudy didn't quite get. He'd fake a laugh like it was the funniest thing he'd ever heard. Not once did Brad remember Rudy ever asking Arnie, or anyone else, to explain what was so darn funny.

As Brad turned to leave the cafeteria, he couldn't resist looking back toward where Paul and Rudy had been sitting. Brad saw that they were both pointing at him – and both were laughing. In an increasing familiar way, Brad started walking toward his English class feeling like he'd just swallowed a snowball from outside.

The cold feeling of rejection didn't subside much in class. Brad was determined not to look at either one of those guys, but he couldn't help noticing that Mrs. Seversen took what looked like a note away from Paul. Brad tried not to think about what was written or drawn about him on that note. Still, he found himself reading the same paragraph from their assigned story three times before he actually understood what was written.

CHAPTER 27
FRIDAY, NOVEMBER 14
EVENING

"Brad, you aren't eating much," said Mrs. Bateman.

"Really?" Brad asked, seemingly unaware.

"Well, normally you'd already be asking for more macaroni and cheese by this time."

"No… I mean, Yeah… I mean it's really good, Mom," he replied, taking a big bite right afterward.

Brad was slightly irritated that his rotten mood had been noticed. He thought he had been doing a reasonably good job of acting like everything was OK. He wasn't surprised to hear his dad ask him a question immediately after he swallowed.

"So, what was the best part of your day?"

Brad looked at Frannie, pretending that the question had been directed at her. Conveniently, she quickly shoved a forkful into her mouth and just shrugged her shoulders at Brad.

Automatically Brad started the same gesture when he turned back to his dad, but the look on his father's face instantly brought to mind the night he had said something about Brad pretending not to know things.

He knew he couldn't pretend that it had been a great day. Several cruddy things came screaming into his mind instantly. He concentrated on what the day had been like. He tried to push the negative memories out of his head. Maybe it wasn't the *best* part of the day, but a decent thought came to him.

"I guess our geography project is coming along pretty well."

"That sounds good," replied his dad. "Tell us about it."

"So, it's a group project," Brad began, then he shot a quick look at Frannie when he processed that he would have to say that Ashley was one of his partners. He figured Frannie would jump all over that.

So rapidly he continued, "We were assigned Costa Rica, and we're finding out all kinds of kind of pretty cool stuff." He took a breath. "Do you know they don't have an army? Plus, the sun rises and sets there the same time every day, all year." Thinking maybe he'd be able to dodge the topic of who he was working with, he spat out, "Plus they have a gazillion kinds of animals, birds, insects, fish – all that kind of stuff."

His dad chuckled as he responded, "I guess you've already learned a lot!"

"Yeah – tons," said Brad.

"So, let me guess," chimed in Frannie snidely, "You're having to do most of the work because the rest of your little quartet of Arnold, Rudolpho, and Curtis McWorthless are too busy messing around?"

"Well, that's a pretty rude name, Frannie," reacted her mom.

Brad expected his dad to chastise Frannie too, but as he tipped his eyes up from where they had instantly dropped upon hearing Frannie's comment, Brad saw his dad looking directly at him.

Gently, Mr. Bateman asked, "What are you thinking right now, Brad?"

Brad's initial impulse was to say something – anything – that would redirect the conversation away from what he was actually thinking. But as he briefly looked up again at his dad, Brad saw something that urged him to spill it out, to tell his family what he truly was experiencing.

"Well, actually…." he started hesitatingly, "I'm not with those guys. I mean we're not in the same group. On the project. In geography."

Brad's eyes quickly toured the table, then briefly looked up at the three family members seated with him. Each of them was looking intently at him.

"I'm in a group with Nathan and Ashley."

Both his parents immediately shot glances at Frannie, as if to ward off any teasing comment. Frannie sat mesmerized, though, continuing to look at her brother.

After a bit of somewhat awkward silence, Mr. Bateman asked, "And that's a good thing?"

"That….?" asked Brad.

"Well, that you're working with Ashley and Nathan rather than the, um, usual guys."

Brad put his chin in his hand. He pondered his dad's question.

After a moment, he said, "I know I'm not supposed to pretend I don't know, but I really don't know."

His dad smiled at him, nodding his head slightly.

After another quiet moment, his dad asked, "What *do* you know, son?"

For the next twenty minutes Brad told his parents and sister about how the last few days of school had gone. About Rudy and Paul pointing at him and laughing at him. How the two of them were passing notes that Ms. Cruz had to take. About how it was kind of nice having Curt and Arnie gone through Wednesday, but then how lousy it was when they came back. How Curt's face was still kind of bruised. How the four guys didn't laugh at Brad like Rudy and Paul had, but how they seemed to constantly be laughing hysterically with each other – especially when Brad was somewhere nearby. How they walked by him, all four in a row, and never once even looked at him. How not one of them had said anything to Brad the last three days. About the times he would feel like somebody was watching him, and when he would look up at least one of the four guys would quickly turn his head like he hadn't been staring at Brad. About how after school they had said - Brad knew it was purposely loud enough so he could hear – that it was going to be so great playing basketball tomorrow morning. Rudy even bragged that he was bringing doughnuts.

"That's really crappy," Frannie said sadly. Brad was surprised when neither parent commented on her word choice.

"I am sorry that I assumed you were still with those losers," she continued. Frannie paused a moment, glancing ever-so-briefly at her parents on either side of her, then louder than before, exclaimed, "I mean just who do these idiotic kumquats think they are?" Dramatically, she added, "This is seriously Crap City!"

"Okay, okay, down girl," Mr. Bateman said. Brad thought he detected a small grin on his dad's face as he said it.

After dinner clean-up, Brad walked up to his room. He thought about what Frannie had said. He first laughed a bit at *how* she had said it. Then he felt kind of good inside that she had come to his defense – instead of blasting him like she often did. But then one comment came back clearly to him: "I assumed you were still with those losers."

Brad clearly wasn't with them in the geography group. But was he not with them…. at all?

CHAPTER 28
SATURDAY, NOVEMBER 3
MORNING

Brad was sound asleep and didn't notice the door to his room being opened. He didn't hear the footsteps crossing toward him either. So, when there was a gentle tap on his shoulder, it took him a moment to actually wake up enough to register that his mom was standing next to his bed. Her typical sunshiny smile was there as always. Brad blinked a couple of times, but neither of them said a word. His mom just stood there all cheery. He was confused why she was there. He hadn't noticed the cordless phone in her hand, then she held it out closer until it was right in front of him.

Still groggy, Brad took a few seconds to pull his hand from under the covers and take the phone. He stared at it, as if the caller could be seen.

He managed to ask, "Who?"

His mom quickly covered the mouthpiece and simply said, "A friend!" Then, grinning broadly, she turned back toward the door.

With droopy eyes, Brad watched her. As she opened the door, his eyes quickly opened much wider as he saw Tripp scrambling around his mom, heading his way. Brad watched as his mom spun delicately away from the charging dog, and in that moment Brad realized where Frannie got her dancing skills.

But he couldn't admire his mom's grace for long because Tripp launched himself on top of the bed, and thus on top of Brad. The phone went flying out of his hand, and Brad struggled to free himself from his covers and the exuberant pet.

Very awake now, Brad loudly commanded, "Tripp, get the heck off me!"

Evidently assuming the push from his master was an invitation to wrestle, Tripp launched into Brad with even more energy, rumbling a playful growl in the process. Tripp's wet slobbery lick right across Brad's lips was the final nudge to get Brad upright and out of bed.

He stood a bit unsteadily a moment, then remembered the phone. He turned to his right and was instantly met face-to-face with the canine, whose tale was wagging at warp speed as he proudly stood on the bed. Brad turned away just as Tripp tried to give him a second kiss, and he spied the phone on the floor.

As he reached for it, he could faintly hear a muffled voice, "Hello? Hello, is Brad there? Brad??"

It dawned on Brad that he still didn't know who was calling. What once were the typical possibilities of Rudy, Curt, and Arnie – in that order – quickly flashed through his mind, each carrying a fleeting mix of hope and regret.

Puzzled, Brad realized that it wasn't very likely that any of those guys would be calling him.

Brad picked up the phone and tentatively said, "Hello?"

"Oh, hi, Brad! It's me, Nathan," came a loud and very enthusiastic response.

"Oh, hey, Nathan," Brad replied, trying not to sound discouraged.

Glancing at his clock, Brad's eyes widened as he realized it was 8:20 – and on a Saturday morning. Jeesh!

He waited for Nathan to say something, anything, before finally asking, "So what are you doing, Nathan?"

"Well…" Nathan began dramatically, before he excitedly continued, "I am calling to give you an invitation!"

Thinking that just maybe Nathan might tell him what the invitation was for, Brad waited. Then he waited some more.

"Brad, are you still there?" Nathan finally asked.

"Uh, yeah, I'm still here, Nathan."

"Oh good."

After another moment of uncomfortable silence, Brad said, "So, um, you called about an invitation?"

"Yes!" Nathan eagerly replied.

Thinking that this was the weirdest phone call he'd ever had, Brad again waited. He was just about to say something, when he heard Nathan quietly talking, apparently with whoever was with him.

"So, yes, Brad," Nathan all but shouted into the phone, "I would like to invite you to come with my father and me to the football game at the college today!"

Amazed at how loud Nathan was, Brad muttered, "Wow."

"Yes, wow!" Nathan enthusiastically yelled. He continued rapidly, "My father says we can pick you up at your home at 12:45. The game doesn't actually start until 2:00, but Father says we should allow time for heavy traffic, then parking, then using the bathroom before finding our seats. Our *reserved* seats," Nathan emphasized.

Feeling almost as blindsided as he had when Tripp pounced on him, Brad wasn't sure what to say.

After a moment, Brad said, "That's very nice of you, Nathan."

"Yes, it is," came the immediate response.

"Um, I'm going to have to talk to my parents." Then realizing this was a done deal in Nathan's mind, Brad added, "Um, I may have to do some work around the house today. But I'll call you back after I talk to them."

"Actually, your mother already told me that you can go with me!" Nathan joyfully announced.

"Oh," Brad said. "She did?"

"Yes, she did!"

Thinking of what it would be like to spend an entire afternoon with Nathan Fenton, Brad stammered quietly, "Wwwwooow."

"Yeah, WOW!" Nathan shouted back.

CHAPTER 29
SATURDAY, NOVEMBER 15
AFTERNOON

Despite several attempts to find something – anything - that he should be doing to help around the house, Brad couldn't convince his parents that he was absolutely needed at home that day. Brad figured they knew right away that he was just trying to get out of going to the game. But he tried anyway.

So it was that at 12:44 he walked to the front of the house. He started to open the door when his dad said, "Wait a second, Brad."

Handing him a ten-dollar bill, his dad said, "I know you'll be polite and appreciative. Use this to buy something for you and Nathan at the concession stand."

Brad put the money in his pocket and said, "Thanks, Dad."

After he walked outside, he turned back and asked, "What about Nathan's dad?"

"Good point!" Mr. Bateman said, chuckling, then reached into his wallet and grabbed $5.

Reaching to give him a hug, Brad's mom said, "Have a great time, sweetie!"

With a bit of a rueful look on his face, Brad thanked her. He turned to the street and as he did so Dr. Fenton pulled up in their van. As Brad climbed in, he noticed the clock on the dashboard read 12:45 exactly.

Nathan was in the second row and Brad thought for a moment about sitting all the way in the back row, but Nathan's huge smile persuaded him otherwise.

After he buckled his seat belt, Brad saw that Dr. Fenton was turned back toward him with his arm outstretched.

Brad shook his hand as he said, "It's good to see you, Brad. Glad you could join us."

"Yeah, thanks for inviting me," came Brad's reply.

"You bet."

Brad sat back in his seat and noticed that Nathan was still just sitting there smiling. Apparently copying his dad, Nathan stuck out his right hand as well. Brad wasn't used to shaking hands with kids his age, but that wasn't the only thing that was different about Nathan. So, he shook his hand and repeated, "Thanks for inviting me."

Nathan quickly said, "You bet."

Brad wondered if it was going to be a copycat deal the entire day. But Dr. Fenton waved to Brad's parents, then pulled out onto Hampshire and didn't say anything more for quite a while.

Nathan asked Brad, "Have you been to any of the football games this year?"

Brad thought a moment before replying, "I guess we haven't gone to any games this year. You?"

"Every one!" came the enthusiastic response.

Nathan continued, "Since Father is a professor at Addams College, we get a good deal on season tickets."

Brad had never thought of Nathan as being much of a sports guy, but he sure knew a lot about the Addams College Eagles football team. He told Brad a lot about the team, including their record, his favorite players – name and jersey number – and he even knew the names of the coaches. It turned out this was a playoff game, and clearly kind of a big deal.

Nathan talked the whole 25-minute drive to the stadium. Other than having to continue turning toward Nathan as he went on, Brad didn't really mind. It kept him from having to say anything.

When they got to the stadium parking lot and got out of the van, Brad noticed Nathan's dad subtly motion his son over to him.

Brad turned away to look at the stadium because he didn't want to be rude.

Right after that Nathan came up to Brad and asked, "So, Brad, what did you do last night?"

Brad was a little surprised because he expected Nathan to tell him more stuff.

He thought for a minute, then said, "Well, after dinner my dad left for a little bit, then when he came back he had a videotape movie."

"I love movies!" Nathan said. He quickly glanced at his dad, then asked, "Um, so what movie was it?"

Brad smiled as he remembered really enjoying the show. "It's called *The Sandlot*," he said. "It was great!"

Nathan said he had seen it a couple of weeks ago. As they walked into the stadium they began talking about the movie. At first Brad kind of resisted laughing, but when Nathan described the scene where the boy pretended he was unconscious, so the cute, older lifeguard would try mouth-to-mouth resuscitation, he couldn't help himself and burst out laughing. As they continued walking, Brad noticed that Nathan was beaming – smiling broadly and looking kind of proud.

As the game went on, Nathan kept an ongoing commentary about what was happening in the game and on the sidelines. Brad noticed that a couple of times Nathan's dad would gently grab his son's knee for a moment, and Nathan would stop talking – but only briefly. Brad mostly watched the game, but there were a lot of other things going on, too, that got his attention. It was a bit confusing trying to be polite and at least nod his head, if not say something, each time Nathan spoke.

Brad remembered the money his dad had given him. In between comments, when Nathan took a breath, Brad jumped right in by asking,

"Want to go get a snack?" Then he quickly added, "My dad gave me some money."

Nathan turned eagerly to his dad, raising his eyebrows in question. His dad merely smiled and nodded his head.

As they both started getting out of their seats, Brad thought to ask, "What would you like, Dr. Fenton? My dad gave me some money."

Dr. Fenton chuckled a bit before replying, "That's very thoughtful of you – and your dad – but I think I'm O.K. Thanks, though!"

The boys walked up the stairs and turned right on the concourse. Brad was surprised there so many people walking around up there, especially considering how many people were sitting in the stands. Nathan obviously knew where he was going, and Brad tried to keep up with him. For every person that was going the same direction, there seemed to be at least two more who were coming at them. At least Nathan was quiet.

As they got near the end of the concourse where it began to curve around the end zone, there was a sudden burst of very loud cheering. Brad stopped, a bit confused. He noticed Nathan jumping up and down in front of him, yelling, "Touchdown! Touchdown, Eagles!"

Just then the band started playing. They were just below the short wall where the boys were standing. And they were loud! Brad stood staring. He was fascinated by the movement of the band members. He counted five trombones, each one of them moving together; turning right, then straight, then left, and never once smacking into each other. He scanned the rest of the band. He counted eight trumpets, and each of them were doing exactly as the trombones. In fact, clarinets, saxophones, and even the small flutes were doing this amazing feat.

Just like that, the band instantly stopped. Brad looked up and realized the team was kicking the extra point after the touchdown. The crowd cheered briefly and not nearly as loudly as a few minutes before.

Brad saw Nathan ahead of him, and he was motioning for Brad to join him. Brad concentrated on working his way around all the people. There were more now who had pushed up against the short wall separating the concourse from the top row of seats, also attracted by the excitement the touchdown had created. Most of the people were taller than Brad. Still, he was able to catch glimpses of Nathan, who thankfully stayed where he was.

A small opening appeared, and Brad moved quickly toward Nathan. Just as he got there a tremendous KABOOM shook the air, the sound way louder than even the band. Brad spontaneously yelled, "AGHHHHHH!" and involuntarily jumped straight up. Nathan burst into laughter, bending over in hysterics. In fact, several others nearby chuckled as well. Brad was completely unsure about what was going on. Still laughing, Nathan couldn't talk. But he pointed toward the back of the end zone. Looking that way, Brad saw the cannon, smoke still coming out from its end. He had forgotten that's how they celebrated touchdowns at Addams College. His mouth still wide open in surprise, Brad looked back to Nathan. He continued cackling. Brad couldn't help himself: he began laughing crazily, too. Any embarrassment he felt melted away, as Brad let himself go. Nathan had tears on his cheeks, he was laughing so hard. Brad felt really good, and he didn't even mind that his ridiculous reaction was the cause of the hilarity. It had been a long time since he had laughed that hard.

As he stepped out of the Fenton's van, Brad looked up to see that both his parents were standing at the front door, smiling and waving. Though he'd already thanked Nathan and his dad, Brad made a point of saying, "Thanks again!" loud enough for his parents to hear, before sliding the van door shut.

"So how was it?" his dad asked, as Brad entered their home.

"It was good. Eagles won," Brad replied as he headed for the kitchen.

They followed Brad, who grabbed an apple and brought it to his mouth in one sweeping motion.

"So you had a good time, sweetie?" his mom cooed.

With his mouth full of apple, Brad simply raised his eyebrows and nodded his head.

On the way home Brad had thought that his mom and dad would probably kind of make a big deal out of him going to the game with Nathan. He knew they had felt bad for him for how things had been going at school. And he did have a good time today. Nathan even talked less in the second half, especially when it got exciting in the 4th quarter.

But still, Nathan was......*Nathan*. Brad didn't want to suddenly be all chummy with the guy.

So, when Brad realized his parents were both standing there expectantly, he strategically said, "I've really got to go to the bathroom!" before taking the stairs two at a time.

CHAPTER 30
THURSDAY, NOVEMBER 20
LUNCH TIME

Bringing his lunch to school four days in a row hadn't really bothered Brad. Even though the pig-in-a-blanket smelled really good, he was relieved to have been able to go straight outside to eat, as he had done all week. He was especially glad the weather had been so nice. As he sat down with his back against the same familiar tree, it dawned on him that Thanksgiving was one week away. He reminisced about several Thanksgivings that had been very snowy. In fact, his grandmother couldn't even make it to their house last year because of a blizzard.

The warmth this year had allowed him to avoid the cafeteria and not have to deal with whatever garbage the four guys would have given him. Brad chuckled to himself when he remembered Frannie saying "Crap City" last week. He wondered if she was aware of the new nickname Ashley and Nathan hinted at for Curt, Rudy, Arnie, and Paul. Of course, none of the three of them said the name aloud in geography class. Brad figured they were being polite. But he also knew that for him at least, he did not want to take any chances that any of the four would hear it aloud. If he thought they were treating him meanly now, just think what it would be like then! Despite the warmth, Brad shuddered.

He thought for a moment and remembered what he felt like last week. As he sat chewing his sandwich, he realized that none of the four boys had done anything that could be considered *mean* this week. They hadn't directed any words or actions to him at all. Where last week they had laughed obnoxiously near him to make him feel left out and traveled down the hall in a line to make a show of ignoring him, this week they just paid no attention to him. It was like he wasn't even visible to them.

Brad wasn't sure which was worse.

Out of nowhere, a football suddenly bounced in front of Brad and nudged his leg. He heard, "Sorry!" before he even saw anyone. Whoever was chasing the ball was silhouetted by the sun as he came to retrieve it. Suddenly the person stopped. He moved to his left, and Brad realized it was Rudy. They both looked at each other, neither one saying anything for a moment.

Finally, Rudy said, "Uh, hey, Brad."

Brad simply replied, "Hey."

Rudy bent down to pick up the ball, looked at Brad briefly, and then took off running slowly in the direction from which he had come.

Brad watched Rudy. When he got closer to the others, Rudy launched the ball toward Arnie. Despite having Curt clinging to his left arm, Arnie made a one-handed catch. A feeling of sadness washed over Brad as he saw the football fly into the air, punted by Arnie to no one in particular but seemingly just for the sake of fun.

CHAPTER 31
FRIDAY, NOVEMBER 21
MORNING

Ms. Cruz got everyone's attention at the start of geography class.

"O.K. people, you all know that we're going to be giving our presentations on Monday and Tuesday."

A few kids groaned, but Ashley, Nathan, and Brad simply looked at each other, smiled, and nodded their heads.

Their teacher continued, "Most of you are in pretty good shape with your projects. But you still need to use the time well today to wrap them up. I believe one or two groups think they're actually done."

At this comment, Brad found himself sinking into his chair a bit because half of the glass groaned this time, and a few even playfully booed.

Ms. Cruz released the class to get to work after having said she wanted to check with the groups who felt like they were done.

Heading straight to the three of them, Ms. Cruz smiled as she said, "So our Costa Rican amigos are thinking they're finished, huh?"

The three smiled, and Nathan handed the packet to her, saying, "Yes, we have completed our work and…" then he paused to glance at his two workmates, "it is…*muy bien.*"

This time Ashley and Brad both groaned.

Ms. Cruz looked through their project, nodding approvingly several times. She agreed they were done, and she complimented them on their work. She told them they could go to the computers at the back of the room and play one of several different geography games.

The three of them excitedly hopped up and headed to the Macintosh computers. As Brad looked up he saw that they were going right by the four guys. None of them looked very happy. At a glance, Brad could tell they were each just copying from an encyclopedia. He knew as soon as Ms. Cruz noticed that she would remind them they had to do more than simply copy.

When Brad sat down at the computer he peeked just past the monitor and saw Rudy looking his way. He didn't look mean or angry. He just looked bummed. Brad quickly turned his attention back to the computer and started up "Cross Country Canada." He figured he'd spent enough time studying Central America and was ready for a trip north. Apparently, Ashley felt the same way because she was already starting the same program on the computer next to him. As he glanced at her, Brad noticed she had her hair pulled back in a ponytail. She looked kind of cute that way, Brad thought. She must have noticed him looking at her because she turned to him, then smiled. At this, Brad flinched then quickly turned to his monitor. He felt his face warm as he blushed a bit.

CHAPTER 32
FRIDAY, NOVEMBER 21
LUNCH TIME

Brad stood in the hot lunch line. He was kind of irritated that it had taken so long to clean up from the experiment in science class. Because of that he was almost at the end of the line. Plus, he was really hungry, and there were at least 20 kids in front of him. He began to wonder if buying pizza was going to be worth it. He looked behind him and there were just three kids. He did a double take as he noticed that Ashley was at the very end of the line. She smiled and waved at him. Brad lifted the right side of his mouth in a half grin and gave a little wave back.

When Brad turned back around he was surprised to see Arnie and the others looking right at him from where they were sitting. Each of them was smiling broadly and waving his hand. Brad was about to wave back when he suddenly realized that they were waving their hands exactly as Ashley had, kind of flapping their fingers. Great! Now they were teasing him, Brad realized.

He instantly looked down. He hoped Ashley wasn't watching, but he was too worried to look up and back at her to check. He didn't want to risk even a slight glance up at the guys to see if they were still waving. His stomach churned.

Brad kept his head down as he shuffled slowly along the pokey line. What was taking so darn long? When it finally was his turn to be served, he looked up and muttered, "Pepperoni, please."

The woman behind the counter gave him an understanding smile, then said, "I am so sorry, but we just ran out. Would you like cheese pizza?"

Brad shook his head, frustrated at how this day had suddenly gone bad.

"Peanut butter and jelly sandwich?" the server asked.

"Uh, no," Brad said. "Pizza."

Then realizing that it wasn't this person's fault they ran out of pepperoni, he managed a soft, "Thanks."

Brad grabbed a carton of milk and did his best to keep his head down as he headed to a table away from the guys. He heard a familiar voice calling, "Brad! Over here! There's room here, Brad!" He looked up to see Nathan waving as if they hadn't seen each other in a week. Nathan scooted over and Brad slipped onto the bench as discreetly as he could. He looked up and nodded at Jermaine, who sat across from him. As soon as he did so, he wished he'd picked that side of the table because just over Jermaine's shoulder the four guys were all looking his way and waving their hands again.

Brad opened his milk carton, just so he had something to do other than think about those jerks.

Nathan said, "Here comes Ashley!"

Brad heard a girl's voice to his left, and he turned to see Sarah Jacobs as she said, "Would you guys mind scooching a little so Ashley could sit by me?"

Overlapping the end of Sarah's question, Brad heard a much louder voice – Arnie – calling toward him mockingly, "Braaad! Oh, Brad, there's room over heeeere!" Then he paused before loudly saying, "Or do you have to sit by your girlfriend?!"

Brad stood up just as Ashley started to squeeze past him toward Sarah. He could hear the raucous laughter coming from Arnie's table. He couldn't help but look that way. The sight of the four bent over in hysterics caused a ribbon of hot anger to instantly shoot through his head. Suddenly the milk carton he'd been holding turned and the cold, white liquid flew through the air and landed right on Ashley's neck.

She shrieked briefly, and the tray she had been holding leapt out of her hands and landed face down on the floor at Brad's feet.

Ashley quickly looked at Brad, her expression a combination of confusion and hurt. Seeming about to cry, she shook her head slightly, then urgently began a rapid walk toward the cafeteria doors.

Brad stood dumbly, his mouth open.

Sarah appeared in front of him, a look of disgust on her face. "Nice job, Brat!" she spat, then turned and quickly followed Ashley.

Still Brad stood, as if frozen. He saw the girls hurry out of the cafeteria, Sarah's arm around Ashley. The laughter he had been dimly aware of suddenly silenced. Seemingly out of nowhere Brad looked up to see Mr. Andrews standing right next to him. His hand came up and landed firmly on Brad's shoulder.

"So what do we have here?" the assistant principal asked, looking at the tray and food scattered on the floor.

Speechless, Brad simply looked up at him.

Abruptly, Nathan stood and rapidly said, "What happened, sir, is that we were trying to make room for Ashley to sit with us, and we were trying to move around, so she could sit next to Sarah, because, well you know they're both girls, and Brad got up and..."

Mr. Andrews interrupted him by calmly saying, "Take a breath and slow down, son."

Nathan literally took a deep breath, then another, before continuing more slowly, "So Brad stood up to allow Ashley to pass, and in the tight space that was created he accidentally spilled his milk on her." Pausing just a moment to look in the direction the girls went, Nathan added, "Clearly this was quite upsetting to our friend."

Deliberately Mr. Andrews looked at Brad, then at Nathan, again down to the mess on the floor, then over to Arnie's table, and finally back at Brad again.

Looking Brad squarely in the eyes, he asked, "Is that what happened?"

Brad involuntarily gulped, then nodded his head once, then a second time.

"Interesting," Mr. Andrews said.

He paused a few moments before adding, "Well maybe you could help by cleaning up this.... accident?"

Brad rapidly nodded his head before bending down to start picking up Ashley's lunch.

CHAPTER 33
FRIDAY, NOVEMBER 21
AFTER SCHOOL

When Brad finally arrived at home he wondered if he would throw-up. He had felt awful the entire afternoon, and he knew that it was more than just the fact that he'd hardly eaten a bite that had caused his nausea. He'd made a snap decision to walk home after school when he saw Curt and Paul by the bike racks. He'd even taken a long way home, going all the way up to Wilmington before heading back on Hampshire. And now he stood in the kitchen, uncertain what to do.

He was relieved to see his mom's note on the message board by the phone telling him she was at the grocery store. He did not want to talk to anyone. He looked at the phone stand and saw the church directory. What seemed like the day's 50th wave of guilt crashed over Brad, and he said softly aloud, "I need to call her."

Just then Tripp barged through the doggie door and barked his happy bark and did his full-body wag. Brad couldn't help but smile at the goofy hound; nothing ever seemed to make him gloomy.

Impulsively, Brad went to the garage and grabbed Tripp's leash. Taking his dog for a walk might help him sort out what to do. Plus, it was long enough after school now that no one would still be there, and he could pick up his bike without seeing anyone. He attached the leash, not a simple chore with the wiggly bouncing dog, then opened the garage door. Holding on tightly to Tripp's leash, he pushed the button to close the door as he raced to get them both underneath it before it shut. Brad stopped in the driveway for a moment. He hadn't noticed after school how much colder it had gotten. He thought about going back inside and grabbing a coat.

"We'll be fast, won't we, boy?" he said to Tripp instead.

As if he understood, Tripp pulled hard on the leash as he headed down the driveway.

They half walked, half ran toward school. Moving fast kept Brad from getting too cold. Moving fast….is what Tripp liked to do. Though he wasn't expecting there to be any kids still at school, Brad was relieved nevertheless to find nobody around. His bike looked kind of lonely standing there by itself. As he bent down to turn the combination lock he was surprised by the sight of snowflakes landing and instantly melting on the asphalt. Brad looked up to see even more snow suddenly falling. It had been quite a while since he had ridden his bike with Tripp, and the change in weather was going to make that even more interesting. Brad pulled the lock out through the back tire and frame then wrapped it around the seat stem. He drew Tripp's leash a little closer to him, pulled the bike away from the rack, and hopped on the seat. Instantly it felt wrong. Brad looked first at the front tire, then quickly to the back. Both were completely flat. The tube stem covers sat on the ground, clear signs of someone intentionally letting air out of each tire.

Frustrated beyond mere words, Brad clenched his fists and let out a primitive growl. He could not believe how this day was going. Knowing that his biggest problem of the day was his fault didn't help his attitude. Anger had overtaken guilt at this point.

Having no other choice, he quickly threaded the caps on the tube stems and began pushing the bike back toward home. Tripp tried to quicken the pace, but Brad pulled hard on the leash and tersely said, "We can't go any faster, Tripp, so just chill out!" Brad shivered, and the irony of the word "chill" dawned on him as he trembled in the increasing cold.

The walk home seemed to take at least three times as long compared to going to school. His sweatshirt was soaked, his hair dripped, and his fingers ached from the cold. Feeling a little bad for acknowledging it, Brad still felt relief that his mom wasn't home yet. He didn't see a light in Frannie's room, and he hoped she still wasn't home either. Just then Tripp shook, and tons of the wet snow that stuck to his fur flew in the air, some landing coldly in Brad's face. He couldn't even respond.

Instead, Brad looped the leash through the frame of the bike, figuring not even Tripp could drag the bike very far. Brad unlocked the front door, went through the kitchen to the garage and opened the big door. He brought Tripp and the bike inside the garage, closed the door, then grabbed a towel to try to dry off the dog as much as possible. Just as he opened the door to the house, he heard the garage door open again. He quickly ushered Tripp inside. Starting to panic a bit, Brad looked around for a clue for what he should do. He looked at the phone and again noticed the church directory. He urgently grabbed it, ran up the stairs, and closed the door to his room. Just as rapidly he opened his door, stepped out into the hall, grabbed the cordless upstairs phone, and dashed into the bathroom. He turned on the shower, figuring his mom would hear it and not come upstairs just yet. A pang of misgiving came over him that he wasn't going to help his mom unload the groceries. But one look at his soggy self in the mirror told him a hot shower was exactly what he should do.

Being in the shower had given Brad time to plan. With a towel wrapped around his waist he had simply hollered hello down to his mom when he was done. He briefly said he had taken Tripp for a walk and got caught in the snow. He told her he'd get dressed and come down in a little bit. Brad took a step toward his room then remembered the phone in the bathroom. He snatched it his right hand and zipped into his room. Brad quickly got dressed in warm sweats, and before he could second guess himself he looked up the Sherman's phone number and dialed it.

Brad expected Mrs. Sherman to answer, so he was taken aback a bit by the sound of Ashley's voice.

"Hello," she said.

"Oh. Um, hi, Ashley," Brad managed.

Silence.

131

"It's me, Brad," he said.

"I know," came the short reply.

"So how are you doing?"

"Better than lunch time."

"Yeah. Um, I bet." He paused. "So, I want to apologize for accidentally spilling the milk on you."

"Accidentally?!" Ashley fiercely replied. "Listen, Brad Bateman, I can handle – maybe – you doing something *stupid*... but I can NOT handle you lying to me!"

"But..." Brad started.

Then pausing a bit, he continued. "I am really, REALLY sorry for spilling the milk on you. It was completely stupid. I am completely stupid!"

"You were stupid, Brad."

"Yeah, I really was," he said quietly.

Neither said anything for a few moments.

Uncomfortable with the silence, Brad stammered softly, "I just..."

"Just what, Brad?"

Brief thoughts of his frustration with Arnie and the others flitted about his head. But Brad pushed them away and instead said, "You did not deserve that, Ashley. That's all. You did nothing wrong. I did something horribly bad to you, and I am very VERY sorry."

"Thank you," she whispered.

Brad thought about saying something about the snow, but that just seemed dumb. He was about to just say goodbye, when Ashley said, "I heard Arnie."

Brad blushed and didn't know what to say.

"You shouldn't let those guys get to you like that," Ashley offered.

"Yeah," Brad replied. "Arnie especially bugs me....so much!" he ended, more excitedly than he intended.

"Thanks for admitting you practically threw milk all over me on purpose," Ashley said, the hint of a slight chuckle in her voice. "You didn't suppress the truth." After a pause, she added, "Eventually."

CHAPTER 34
MONDAY, NOVEMBER 24
LUNCH TIME

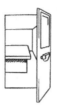

Brad opened his thermos, and as he began to drink the milk inside, he stopped a moment. He thought how different it was today compared to the last time he had a milk container in his hand at school. He didn't mind sitting by himself in the conference room in the office. He didn't even care that Mr. Andrews chose lunch time to respond to the note Brad had written to him and delivered before school. Following the assistant principal into his office with all the kids around was embarrassing. But Brad figured he deserved it.

It had even surprisingly worked out okay when Arnie yelled, "You gonna drench your woman again today, Brat Ratman?!" right as Mr. Andrews appeared.

He had calmly looked at Arnie and said, "I look forward to our visit later today, Mr. Sutter."

Looking completely clueless, Arnie nervously asked, "What visit?"

"Why, the one you just invited yourself to with that rude outburst," Mr. Andrews replied with a sarcastic grin.

It certainly was not easy looking directly at the assistant principal and apologizing for lying to him. Mr. Andrews clearly wasn't thrilled to hear that. But when he learned that Brad had written the note asking to see him on his own without his parents prompting him, he seemed kind of impressed. Brad's parents complimented him a little bit for that, too. Well, after they told him he was grounded to his room for the weekend.

Of course, he did get out of the house to go to church. Sunday School was rough. Brad had also told his parents that he would admit lying to the whole group before either his mom or dad even mentioned it. He was sure Nathan was going to wet his pants when Brad came right out and said he intentionally spilled the milk on Ashley. When Brad said he then lied about it when Mr. Andrews asked if it was an accident, a squeal of fright burst out from Nathan. Brad assured him that he would make sure that Mr. Andrews knew that Nathan completely believed it had been an accident. That seemed to help a little, but Nathan squirmed for the next 10 minutes regardless. Brad had actually managed to joke a bit that he wondered if he'd get extra homework credit in Sunday School for having had a second discussion with his parents about honesty. He told the group that he promised his parents that he would never suppress the truth again.

Ashley had patiently and quietly sat throughout Brad's explanation, even though everyone turned to look at her when Brad had revealed the truth. She couldn't quite completely suppress a giggle when Nathan let out his squeal, though. After Pastor Dan skillfully thanked Brad for his honesty without approving his lying, Ashley raised her hand.

"I know you're probably wondering what I think about all this," she calmly started. "Well…. it was COLD, UNEXPECTED, and really, truly, LOUSY!" she exclaimed, giving Brad a funny, whacky look. She laughed a bit, which allowed everyone else to join her.

"And just so everyone knows, Brad *maturely* called me to apologize for his *immaturity* before he talked to anyone else." Brad looked up and gave a slight smile.

"And did I mention it was EMBARRASSING?!" Ashley continued.

"And that is why I would *love* it if this topic could just kind of die away. My feelings will not be hurt if no one," and she gave Sarah a brief smile, "NO one, ever says anything to me to try to 'make it better'."

She paused a moment, then completed her thoughts, "It was dumb, it wasn't fun, but it's over. O-V-E-R." She looked like she was going to say more, but Ashley simply smiled and said, "Thanks."

As Brad re-lived that experience, the door to the conference room opened. Mrs. Johnson poked her head in and said, "Lunch time is over, Brad. It's time to head to your fifth period class."

CHAPTER 35
WEDNESDAY, NOVEMBER 35
AFTERNOON

Despite the cold air, Brad felt good inside. The snow that had started last Friday and had continued off and on over the next four days, seemed to finally be gone. The sun was shining, and the sky was incredibly blue. Brad carried his plastic Snow Disk and walked up by the flag pole in front of their school where Jermaine, Nathan, Sarah, and Ashley waited for him.

Following his time in the office, the rest of Monday afternoon and all of Tuesday had gone relatively well. He, Ashley, and Nathan got an "A" on their geography presentation. He and Ashley really didn't say much to each other. Brad had noticed that the four guys each had been placed in four separate corners of the room during the presentations. Brad tried hard not to ever look at any of them. However, Nathan had, and he conspiratorially told his two teammates that the boys each had an individual packet of worksheets they were assigned to do since they didn't finish their research project. But school was out for five days of Thanksgiving break now. Brad was thrilled about that and didn't want to think any more about school until he had to.

This sledding trip apparently had been Ashley's idea. She first called the others Sunday afternoon, but Brad was still grounded and couldn't take the call. Ashley later told Brad that his mom could not stop apologizing about the milk incident, even offering to buy Ashley two new shirts because "the original shirt just had to be ruined!"

Brad was somewhat nervous about how it would go being with these four kids. Even though he knew them all from church, they really had never done anything on their own together. It was true that Ashley had invited him, but he still wondered if she would be upset with him. She had given him a brief smile when Brad had walked up and had simply said, "Hi" before grabbing her inner tube and heading down the front sidewalk.

She and Sarah led the way, crossing Mae Boulevard and heading south. Nathan didn't seem to quite know where he fit, and he ended up kind of between the girls and the end of the group where Jermaine and Brad walked. Jermaine started talking right away. He was funny, too. At one point the other three in front stopped and turned around to see what made Brad laugh so hard. He told Jermaine to repeat his impersonation of Mr. Andrews, and he gladly did, mimicking the administrator's deep voice effectively and even somehow seeming to stand taller as he firmly put his hand on Brad's shoulder just like had happened at school. Ashley and Sarah had already left the cafeteria and hadn't seen that exact encounter, but they'd seen Mr. Andrews enough times before and they laughed hard, too, at Jermaine's accurate portrayal. Brad had even briefly felt some of the same fear that he had on Friday.

As they continued to walk, the five talked more as a group. They agreed to sled down the south side of Harrelson Hill. It wasn't as steep as the east side, but that slope ended up in a flat part of the park, whereas on the east side there wasn't much landing space before Mae Boulevard.

They weren't the only people who thought sledding would be a good idea. As they approached the park they could hear the screams and laughter before they even saw anyone. Brad flashed back in his mind to a day last year when he was with Arnie, Curt, and Rudy. The four boys had always gone on the south hill before, but that day Arnie decided they were big enough to take on the steeper hill. The screams Brad now heard as they approached the park took him right back to last year. He remembered the look of terror on Curt's face as he had zoomed down the icy hill, out of control and petrified.

Ashley, Sarah, Jermaine, Nathan and Brad approached the same base of the east side of the hill that Brad had just been picturing. Brad was looking down, trudging through the snow piled up in their path. Suddenly Sarah hollered, "Stop!", panic evident in her voice. The other four quickly looked up in surprise as a group of three high school aged kids came flying wildly down the hill on a toboggan. Screaming hysterically, they seemed to have no control at all as they zipped crazily down the hill. Unexpectedly each of them launched off the sled as they approached the street. The toboggan continued, not slowing a bit. A kaleidoscope of hurtling arms, legs, and puffs of snow erupted as the kids landed and rolled. The toboggan shot across Mae, bouncing erratically as it hit bumps, then the curb, before eventually slowing as it slid up a slight incline on the other side of the road. It glided down a bit before coming to rest, the back half sticking out into the street. The now snow-covered riders laughed and exchanged low fives in celebration.

Brad and the others watched the scene, somewhat in disbelief. After a long silence, Nathan said what they probably all were thinking, "Wow, if they stayed on that toboggan and a car came driving by......Wow!" After a moment, they started to once again cross the base of the steep hill.

Without warning, a shrieking yell assaulted their ears. They looked up and saw a single rider on a sled heading right at them. Nathan, Sarah, and Jermaine immediately turned around and did their best to hurry out of the way. Ashley dropped her inner tube and tried to run forward. Brad took a step to follow her, then halted when he heard the bellowing shout more clearly as it neared, "RAAAAAAT-MANNNNNNN!"

Brad froze in his tracks as he focused on the shape barreling toward him. In an instant of recognition, it made no sense and at the same time it made perfect sense: It was Arnie, hurtling toward him, absolutely out of control, but speeding at him nonetheless. Brad shot a quick glance to the street and saw a car heading south. Brad took one step back and timed his leap, hoping that he was lucky. The collision with Arnie was painful. It knocked him off his sled, and Brad landed awkwardly on top of him. The force of the impact forced a loud grunt out of Arnie, followed by a piercing yell of agony. From the ground, Brad looked toward the street just in time to see the sled demolished into pieces as the car crashed into it, the driver obviously never seeing it as it sailed into the road.

Brad flopped onto his back, letting out a huge breath of air. He was partially aware of voices and movement, but mostly he looked at the sky. It was such an amazing, beautiful blue. That's the only thing Brad was aware of for quite a while.

CHAPTER 36
THURSDAY, NOVEMBER 27
THANKSGIVING DAY

As Brad set the silverware on the table, remembering to put the knives and spoons on the right and the forks on the left side of the plates, he stopped and looked around. He gazed into the living room. His grandma and Mrs. Chestler sat in the corner, chatting away, seemingly unaware of anyone else. Brad was glad that the roads had cleared enough for his grandma to join them this year. He thought for a moment that if any of the three pies that Mrs. Chestler had brought were even partly as good as her pumpkin bread, then Brad figured he wouldn't need to eat anything else.

He turned his attention to the kitchen. Thinking she was so sneaky that no one would notice, Frannie dipped a spoon into the whipped cream container and put a huge mound of it into her mouth. Rolling her eyes in delight, she quickly scooped another bite before slipping it back into the refrigerator.

His dad stood at the stove, a wooden spoon in one hand and a lid in the other. Brad knew he was fiddling with the mashed potatoes, making sure that his one contribution to the meal preparation was just right. He stepped to the spice cabinet, and almost simultaneously Brad's mom slid to where her husband had just stood and opened the oven door. She put on oven mitts and pulled the roasting pan partway out. She checked the thermometer and, satisfied, hoisted the heavy turkey up onto the counter where a cutting board awaited. Brad wondered who weighed more, that big bird or his mom.

Just then the phone rang. Of course, Frannie all but hurled herself toward it.

"Happy Thanksgiving," she practically sang as she answered the call.

"Well, actually we're about to eat...." she said, with much less enthusiasm. "But, I guess if it's quick it will be alright."

She held out the phone to Brad without saying anything.

Brad took the phone and tentatively said, "Hello?"

"First of all," the somewhat croaky voice began, "I want you to know this was not my idea. My mom is making me do it."

Brad realized it was Arnie.

"Okay..." Brad said.

"So anyway," Arnie continued, "you remember when we were in third grade?"

Confused, Brad slowly said, "Uh, yeah I do remember third grade." He paused, then added, "What about it?"

"Remember having chicken fights?" Arnie asked.

"Yeah, I guess so."

"I guess you remember that you broke your wrist?"

"Yeah, I definitely remember that *you* broke my wrist," Brad replied with some irritation.

"So, yeah, well, now we're even."

It took Brad a moment to figure out what Arnie meant. When it dawned on him, he said, "Your wrist is broken?"

"Yep, got a cast on it last night," Arnie proudly said.

"And that happened yesterday.... while you were, um, sledding?"

"Yep. You put a pretty good hit on me," Arnie said.

"I am kind of sore," Brad replied, holding the phone between his ear and neck so he could rub his right shoulder.

"So anyway, my mom says I should thank you."

There was a pause.

"She saw the sled – or what was left of it – when she came to take me to the doctor. She said that could have been me."

Brad wasn't sure what to say. After a few moments, he hesitantly said, "You're welcome."

Now it was Arnie's turn to pause.

"So, um... well, I guess we're done here."

142

Wondering if that meant they were done *now,* or done, done, Brad responded, "Yep, I think we are done."

He looked at the phone, questioning if the call was over. He heard a click and got his answer.

Brad put the phone back on the cradle and turned around.

He stood a moment, trying to understand what just happened. He hadn't tried to hurt Arnie; just the opposite. He felt some remorse that Arnie's wrist was broken. But at least he was better off than his sled! Arnie had thanked him. Well, kind of. What had he said? His *mom* wanted him to call to thank Brad. Then Arnie had said "We're done here."

Clearly the phone call was done. Brad pondered again whether Arnie meant that their long-time friendship was over, too. A momentary wave of sadness passed through Brad. Almost immediately, though, the melancholy was gone. Brad realized if this meant that they wouldn't have anything to do with each other, he was okay with that. In fact, he felt peaceful inside.

Brad suddenly became aware that it was very quiet. He looked up from where he had been staring at the floor. Everyone was looking at him, curiosity etched on each face.

Brad looked from person to person. Then a funny half chuckle burst out from him. A tremendous sense of relief engulfed Brad.

Not knowing what else to do, he loudly said, "I love Thanksgiving! I'm starving….so let's eat!"

The others began laughing. His grandma and Mrs. Chestler began heading to the table, followed by Frannie. His dad reached for a knife and began cutting the turkey. His mom appeared at the table with a bowl of sweet potatoes. Brad breathed in deeply, enjoying the pleasant sensation. He practically glided into his chair. A comforting surge of thankfulness swept through him, as he eyed the table full of food and the people around it. He didn't even try to suppress the huge smile spreading across his face.

 **ABOUT THE ARTIST**

Jackson Aldern was born and raised in Fort Collins, Colorado. Since receiving his Bachelor's of Fine Arts in painting and graphic design from Colorado State University, he has been working as a designer and full-time artist. Passions of Jackson's include backpacking, reading, and playing music. See his portfolio at www.JacksonAldern.com.

Made in the USA
Monee, IL
11 November 2019